WORTH A FORTUNE

Praise for Sam Ledel

Rocks and Stars

"I think Sam Ledel told a great story. I adored Kyle even though a few times I wanted to shake her and say enough, girlfriend. I wish the ending was a bit longer, but that's the romance addict in me. I look forward to Ledel's next book."
—*Romantic Reader Blog*

The Princess and the Odium

"The world-building in the whole trilogy is fantastic, and even if it feels familiar now that we've been navigating it with the characters for a while, it's still surprising and unsettling. All in all, *The Princess and the Odium* is a fitting end to a well-written YA fantasy series."—*Jude in the Stars*

Broken Reign

"Sam Ledel has created a fascinating and at times terrifying world, filled with elves, sirens, selkies, wood nymphs and many more...Going on this journey with both young women and their fellow travellers still has this fresh and exciting quality, all the more so as new characters joined the story, some just as intriguing."—*Jude in the Stars*

Daughter of No One

"There's a lot of really smart fantasy going on here...Great start to a (hopefully) long running series."—*Colleen Corgel, Librarian, Queens Public Library*

"It's full of exciting adventure and the promise of romance. It's sweet, fresh and hopeful. It takes me back to my teenage years, the good parts of those years at least. I read this in a few hours, only stopped long enough to have lunch. I hope I won't have to wait too long for the sequel—I have high hopes for Jastyn, Aurelia, their friend Coran, Eegit the hedgewitch and Rigo the elf."—*Jude in the Stars*

"A fantasy book with MCs in their very early twenties, this book presents a well thought out world of Kingdom of Venostes (shades of The Lord of the Rings here)."—*Best Lesfic Reviews*

"Sam Ledel has definitely set up an epic adventure of star-crossed lovers. This book one of a trilogy doesn't leave you with a cliffhanger but you are definitely going to be left ready for the next book...As a non-fantasy lover, I adored this book and am ready to read where Ledel takes us next. This book is quality writing, great pacing, and top-notch characters. You cannot go wrong with this one!"—*Romantic Reader Blog*

"If you're a huge fan of fantasy novels, especially if you love stories like this one that contains a host of supernatural beings, quirky characters coupled with action and excitement around every tree, winding path or humble abode, then this is definitely the story for you! This compelling story also deals with poverty, isolation and the huge chasm between the royal family and the low-class villagers. Well, fellow book lovers, it really looks like you've just received a winning ticket to a literary lottery."—*Lesbian Review*

By the Author

Rocks and Stars

Wildflower Words

Worth a Fortune

The Odium Trilogy

Daughter of No One

Broken Reign

The Princess and the Odium

Visit us at www.boldstrokesbooks.com

WORTH A FORTUNE

by
Sam Ledel

2022

ISBN 13: 978-1-63679-175-3

This Trade Paperback Original Is Published By
Bold Strokes Books, Inc.
P.O. Box 249
Valley Falls, NY 12185

First Edition: July 2022

CREDITS
EDITOR: BARBARA ANN WRIGHT
PRODUCTION DESIGN: STACIA SEAMAN
COVER DESIGN BY JEANINE HENNING

Acknowledgments

Thank you to the entire Bold Strokes Books team. Thank you to my editor, Barbara Ann Wright, who helped point out those sneaky anachronisms.

A special thanks to my family for their love and support in this writing journey.

For those lucky enough to have found their own reunion romance.

PROLOGUE

1939, Manhattan, New York

Beneath the large black umbrella, Harriet Browning stood beside her mother in the Trinity Church cemetery as her father's casket was lowered into the damp earth. She stared at its gleaming edges, the rain sliding off in slick turrets. All around them, nearly a hundred people in dark coats, fine hats, and polished shoes stood beneath their own umbrellas. It would be useless, she knew, to search for Ava. She hadn't seen her in years; why would she show up now after what Harriet did?

"Do you believe what she's wearing?" Harriet's mother asked. "You'd think we were at the World's Fair, not my husband's funeral."

Harriet shot her mother a look from behind her netted veil. She followed her mother's light blue eyes to Mrs. McCarthy standing opposite the gravesite. She was indeed wearing an elaborate outfit, some sort of robe-meets-cape ensemble. Harriet admired her shimmering, star-shaped brooch that glistened amid the gray, midmorning air. Rain fell steadily over the cemetery, streaming off surrounding tombstones, the polished rocks shedding their own sympathetic tears.

She leaned closer beneath their shared umbrella. "Don't you mean ex-husband, Mother?"

Velma Browning, regal as ever in an elegant black dress that covered every part of her trim figure from her neck to her ankles and was accented in black lace, waved a silk handkerchief at Harriet. She dabbed her mascara-coated eyes and rouged cheeks in lieu of a reply.

"How is Bob, anyway? I thought he might have accompanied you."

"He's at the ranch. He's meeting me in Nebraska when I head back. And his name, as you are well aware, is Buck."

"Buck is something you hunt, Mother. Not someone you marry."

Her mother sniffled as the minister continued a prayer. "Just wait until you meet him, sweetheart."

"And when will that be?"

"We plan to visit after the honeymoon, darling. I'll telephone with the date once things are settled."

Settled. Harriet hadn't felt settled in a long time. When was the last time her life had felt right? Felt content? A flash of memory sprang into her mind as she stared at the water sticking in droplets to the grass: sunny skies, a black iron table littered with the remnants of sweet coffee and pastries. Her mother and father chatted as she sat opposite them in a Paris café.

Harriet blinked. She'd been fifteen. God, was that really the last time she'd felt happy?

Another memory flared: a dimly lit dorm room, a shared glass of wine, and Ava lounging in her robe at the end of their bed. That, Harriet thought with a sharp inhale, was happiness.

Many of the funeral-goers wore dark glasses. The elite of New York had gathered to witness one of their own venture to his rest. She knew, though, what really drove them here, and it wasn't sadness or grief. Harriet could feel what it really was trickling down the blades of green, climbing across the muddy ground, and tiptoeing around the six-foot-deep hole.

They weren't just there to say good-bye to Charles M. Browning. No. They were there to see her. To see how the only daughter of the Browning timber fortune would handle herself at a time like this.

She glanced around, grateful for the veil of water falling steadily that helped shield her gaze. Grace Vanderbilt gave her a sympathetic frown. Grace's father, Brigadier General Cornelius Vanderbilt, stood beside her, muttering to Jack Morgan. Harriet imagined they were already discussing who would come after the Browning assets first now that her father was gone.

She felt small, as if she was nine and not a woman in her mid-twenties. She prided herself on being capable, independent, and well-versed in her role in life. But that life had always contained her father, even if he had been more of a fleeting presence than a constant figure. He had been a kind, hardworking man. He'd made sure she wanted for nothing. Affection was likened to material comforts. In that way, Harriet knew, he had loved her. And despite only catching glimpses of him behind his office door most of her life or stealing a hug before he caught another train to visit a mill, she had loved her father deeply. Now, even that ephemeral occurrence was gone. Now, half of New York's high society watched her, daring her to cry, willing her to crumple under this new absence. It made her dizzy.

"Mother." Harriet turned, adjusting the umbrella as the minister finished his prayer. His monotonous voice struggled to carry over the rain. She searched for her mother's eyes behind the heavy black veil.

Her mother was checking her watch, and Harriet grimaced,

knowing she was already mentally packing for her train ride west. "Yes, darling?"

Harriet wanted to ask, "What do we do now?" She wanted to talk to her mother, hug her, let herself cry. But then, she wouldn't be Harriet Browning if she did. "Nothing."

Several people cried out as the gravedigger shoveled the first layer of dirt over the coffin. As the hard earth hit the wood, Harriet steeled herself. It would be up to her to maintain face among these people. She would have to carry on her family's place in the world. She dragged her gaze across the sea of black. All eyes searched her for a hint of emotion, a crack in the facade of the mourning heiress, something signifying another family had fallen in America's shrinking aristocracy.

Pulling back her shoulders, Harriet took one more look at her father's headstone. Then she turned. "Let's go, Mother," she said, and led them to the car.

CHAPTER ONE

1948, New York City

"Don't forget this."

Ava Clark turned, teetering slightly as the box containing her desk items shifted, threatening to pull her sideways behind her now empty desk. Her best friend, Imogene, held up a silver inkwell and pen. It had been a gift from the main postal office in London to commemorate her contribution to the war effort. Imogene dropped the set carefully into the box, then grabbed her own items.

"Thanks."

Most of the mail-sorting room had been cleared out. The desks were empty, and chairs littered the large room now that the three dozen sorters were no longer needed. Over the last few days, they'd been sent home in waves. Today, it was Ava's turn. She'd known this day was coming, but like all inevitable endings, it had still snuck up on her, seeming to have happened slowly and all at once, spinning her mind into a frenzy with this new reality. The reality that she was undoubtedly unemployed.

A few ladies lingered near the back of the room, smoking and sharing a flask. They all wore similar outfits to Ava and Imogene, who was making a last-ditch effort to push in chairs.

All the women wore pants boasting gloriously wide pockets and billowy legs paired with sleek, button-down blouses. Like Ava, her now-former colleagues wore their hair swept back from their faces. Their ends were either gently curled, or the front was twirled and pinned behind their ears in a flattering way, much like Ingrid Bergman or Greta Garbo. Ava liked to model hers after Jane Wyman and how she wore it when she'd married that actor, Reagan Somebody, in 1940.

Unlike the other women, though, Ava only wore a light pink lipstick compared to their thickly coated lashes and cheeks. She'd never understood the appeal of covering her face in paint only to take it off each night and reapply the next morning. This was something she and Imogene often agreed to disagree on.

Outside the old brick office building, the unusually stifling April air hit Ava like a wall. The bottom of one of her shoes stuck to a piece of gum on the sidewalk. She tugged herself free, scraping her two-inch heel on the curb as Imogene joined her. Even at six o'clock, the weight of what would be a gruesome summer in New York City was crippling.

"Wanna come over?" Imogene balanced her box under one arm in order to swipe a piece of bleach-blond hair from her sticky forehead. Her blue eyes stood out beneath eyeshadow and a healthy layer of mascara. "Joe's got a six-pack cooling."

Ava considered a night on her friend's fire escape. They could bemoan the end of their time with the War Department's fifty-third annex for the United States Postal Service until the stars mingled with the city lights.

The war had been over for more than two years, but the postal service had been integral in tracking down lost or wounded soldiers and reuniting families in the toilsome aftermath. For whatever reason, the government deemed now the time to begin giving up on those remaining missing souls and shutting down half the offices across the country. Ava needed to process such a change alone. At least, for now.

"I'll pass," she said, waving to hail a cab that sped by, ignoring her raised hand. "Gotta get home." She smiled as she hitched up the box against her hip. Fading evening light ricocheted off the looming office buildings and warehouses that lined the crowded street. She was grateful when Imogene only nodded and managed to hail a cab within seconds. They'd been friends since college, and Imogene knew her well enough to know when she needed time to herself. Even if that time boasted only a sad potted plant and a nearly empty fridge for comfort at her apartment in Brooklyn. Still, the frenetic pace of the last week—all of her office let go, their services no longer needed now that the final wave of soldiers was coming home—had taken its toll.

"I'd say see you tomorrow, but I guess that won't happen," Imogene called as she shoved her things into the cab's back seat.

"I'll call you," Ava replied, waving as Imogene climbed in and disappeared into the sea of cars.

Three attempts later, Ava managed to catch a cab home. Her apartment building was nondescript, shabby, and hosted a layer of soot and grime like many of the other buildings on the block. A rusty fire escape snaked its way up the left side, overlooking a crowded alley. She caught the street-level door with her foot behind Mr. Alcala, who lived in 5B. He was a quiet man with four cats. Ava lugged her box up to the third floor by herself, not completely surprised Mr. Alcala didn't offer to help. She tiptoed past Mr. Wakowski's unit. The landlord was notoriously nosy. He'd have a field day with her box of pencils, paperweights, and memorabilia from the now defunct war-correspondence sorting room.

Her tongue between her teeth, she found her keys and

unlocked her apartment door, slipping inside. Placing the box on her small pale yellow kitchen table, she went straight to the fridge.

"Thank God." There was still a glass of Pinot next to a carton of eggs. Those and a slab of cheddar cheese were the only residents on the shelf.

Ava poured the wine into a chipped mug and started her gas stove. Cracking two eggs, she let the yolks crackle in the pan that lived on the right burner. She took a long sip, closing her eyes.

What would happen now that she was without work? She scrambled her dinner, then tossed the eggs onto a plate and took it with her to the living room five steps away.

A tattered recliner she'd been given by the elderly woman downstairs wobbled when she plopped into it. She didn't bother turning on the lamp atop her side table. The streetlights provided the perfect dimness. Ideal for self-pity, she thought. Across the room, three photos sat in black frames next to an old radio on a card table. Her parents stood beside her in one, both donning solemn smiles as she held a suitcase. Her house and the barn were behind them, rows of corn caught in the freeze-frame. It was taken the day she left for college at Briarcliff, the start of her life in New York.

The other two photos were headshots of her brothers in their respective military uniforms. Her oldest brother, William, had enlisted one year before she went to college. Their mother had wept for a week when he'd told them all one Sunday at dinner. He'd done well in the Army, making first lieutenant and eventually being stationed in Egypt with his own troops to command. Only after the Italian forces invaded that part of the world did she and her parents learn he had been part of Operation Compass, where he'd been killed in the first weeks of fighting in December of 1940.

Her gaze slid to the other photo where her middle brother, James Henry, smiled in his Navy jacket, even though she was certain he'd been told not to smile. He was the spitting image of her father with his hazel eyes, slightly large nose, but otherwise handsome features. He'd enlisted in 1941. Ava had expected more tears from her mother, but James's news had been met with resigned silence. James had been stationed somewhere in northern England. That was 1944.

She and James had dreamed of leaving their family's farm when they were younger. William had always intended to stay, to follow in their father's footsteps and run the farm. But the threat of the Axis powers had called him to action, which had a domino effect on the rest of the Clark children.

All three of them had managed to get out of Pennsylvania. Now, she was the only one left.

Finishing off her eggs, Ava leaned back, the plate in her lap. She swept her gaze over her apartment, listening to the steady hum of the fridge beneath the sounds of the city outside. A thousand thoughts tore through her mind. She needed a job. She needed money. Leaving home all those years ago, she had been determined to make it in the city. She and her brothers had been driven out into the world to make a difference. She'd made a promise to herself a long time ago to make something of her life, to prove she could live on her own. Running back to the comfort of her childhood home wasn't an option. She couldn't bear the looks of disappointment on her parents' faces.

Throwing back the last of her wine, Ava sighed. Staring at the photos, she muttered, "What now, you two? What in the world do I do now?"

CHAPTER TWO

The glaring ring of the bedside phone tore Harriet from her sleep. She bolted up, searching the silk bedsheets, then the air, for the receiver. Blinking around the dark room, she finally found the table and the ornate, bulky telephone. "Hello?"

"Good, you're up. I'm coming by at two today, after I stop by Barneys. They just put out their latest catalog. Have you seen it? There's a wombat collar in there I simply must have."

Harriet fell back into the pile of pillows against her towering mahogany headboard. Adjusting the strap of her negligee, she listened as her friend Scarlett Sachs paused between descriptions of hosiery.

"You there, honey? Or am I talking to the operator again?" Her Southern drawl—faded significantly since Harriet first knew her—pitched lower in concern.

"I'm here." Harriet clicked on her lamp. The soft light barely filled a corner of the cavernous room, gently falling over pink carpet and high white walls.

"Well, get moving, H. It's already after nine. I'll see you at two."

The line went static, and Harriet replaced the receiver. With a sigh, she stretched and went to the west-facing windows. She opened the heavy, patterned drapes, grimacing at the bright April day. Skyscrapers filled her eyeline, familiar as friends. More of them over the last year. Below, on Fifth Avenue, cars and people wove between one another like intricately orchestrated machine parts. The city's pulse beat on as she gazed upon it from behind the thick glass.

Down the hallway, she passed three guest bedrooms lining the left side. She kept the doors closed and the hall lights off. At the end next to the main elevator, she took a right into the entryway that opened to the kitchen.

Harriet prepared breakfast like she did each morning: a hardboiled egg, a piece of toast with marmalade, two celery pieces, and half a cup of grapefruit juice. Arranging the items on a silver tray, she shuffled into the adjoining pantry that connected to the small breakfast room. Sitting at the edge of a bench behind a gleaming wooden table, she mentally prepared for another day. The quiet of living alone settled around her, the gentle sounds of her home a well-worn blanket, one she had worn daily for several years now. She threw a glance to the large windows before refocusing on her food. For only a moment, the sights and sounds of the outside world roared in her mind. Harriet leaned back, closing her eyes to gather herself. She forced the sounds—more memories at this point but sharp and still tangible—to the other side of the window. The roar quelled its temper, and she breathed deeply to quiet her nerves.

A large wall clock chimed the half hour. Harriet finished her meal, strolled through the dining room and gallery, then found the daily paper waiting for her on the private landing next to the elevator. She smiled. The doorman, Bert, had placed the Business pages on top for her again. Pleased, she carried the paper back down the hallway and into the master sitting room, which was on the other side of her dressing room and bathroom, connected through adjoining French doors.

She opened the curtains. Eastern sunlight poured in. Deciding to stay in her robe, she fell onto the burgundy chaise to read.

She was still in the sitting room after several hours passed, and the elevator rumbled to life on the other side of the apartment. Two minutes later, her former sister-in-law, and now dear friend, Scarlett, appeared in the doorway.

"God, H, you didn't want to turn on the lamps? It's as grim as a graveyard in here."

Harriet gestured to the floor to ceiling windows behind her. Afternoon light filled the room, making every piece of polished furniture and even the fireplace mantel gleam. "I don't know what you mean."

Scarlett gave her a look as she removed her fur-trimmed coat, revealing a stunning, vertically striped dress that made her tall, ballerina figure appear even slimmer. Paired with blue heels to match the dress, Scarlet looked impeccable as always. The way Harriet used to be.

"You're early," she added as Scarlett placed her hat, gloves, and handbag on the coatrack. She pushed back her long blond hair that was pulled behind her ears by jeweled pins.

"Hardly," she replied, her deep red-shaded lips lifting in a smile. Her blue eyes grew concerned. "I'm glad I came when I did."

Harriet felt her friend's gaze, so she focused on the article in front of her.

"H, I was abroad for only six months. Your letters were quite convincing. I should have known. You've had a knack for putting up a front since my dear brother was courting you. But truly, dear." She gestured to Harriet's robe and slippers, letting the question hang between them.

"I'm fine," Harriet answered. "It's Friday, Scar. I'm taking it easy."

Scarlett's penciled brow quirked. "Your letters said you've been seeing to your family's affairs."

"I have." She glanced up. "How was Spain, by the way? I want to hear all about it."

She ignored Harriet's attempt to deflect the conversation. "You're going to meetings with your father's advisors?"

She flicked the newspaper page. "They come here."

Scarlett smoothed the lap of her dress as she took a seat in a large leather chair. She scanned the room before saying, "Did you hear, that show that opened on Broadway in February... what was it? *Doctor Social*, it closed three days after opening night. Sylvia saw it. She said it was a bore."

Harriet studied the Tiffany lamp next to Scarlett. It had been her grandmother's. She briefly contemplated how much it might be worth now.

"H?"

"Hmm?" She'd been lost in memories of the last meeting with her father's colleagues and the intimidating stack of documents sitting in the office next door. "Oh, I read the review in the paper. Not surprised it closed."

Scarlett's ankle bobbed as she crossed her legs. Harriet knew that question was Scar's way of asking the last time she'd left the apartment. Broadway used to be like a religion to Harriet.

"I went to the park last week," she decided to say. She had, but only for five minutes before she'd returned to her building, leaving that month's grocery list with the doorman, Bert. He'd had everything delivered by that afternoon.

"Your mother call lately?" Scarlett's smile returned, seeming to take her response in stride. "I miss that woman."

Harriet snorted. "She called three days ago in between hunts with Brad. My mother hunts now," she added sardonically.

"I thought his name was Buck?"

Harriet shrugged. "She sounded happy."

"Good for her. Everyone's hoping she comes back for the fundraiser in September. You know, the one the McCarthys put on each Labor Day?"

"You'll have to tear her away from the cattle."

Scarlett laughed. "I'll phone her. It'll be a grand time."

Harriet moved to stand. "I should mark that date."

Scarlett stood quickly. "You sit. You look like you need the rest." She pursed her lips. "I mean that in the nicest way, H." She disappeared into the office, then returned with a pad of legal paper and a fountain pen. Handing it to Harriet, she said, "That room looks like my father's attorney's office come tax season."

Harriet wrote, *September 6, 1948—McCarthy Fundraiser.* Scarlett moved to look out the window. Turning, she said, "You know I'd help with that, H." Harriet followed her finger that pointed to the office. "If I had the slightest head for it. George handles those things for us." She lifted her shoulder slyly. "Afraid I'm not as modern a woman as I'd hoped to be. Not like you."

In her mind, the stacks of documents seemed to climb higher, pushing against the ceiling. They shot skyward like the buildings outside. Harriet blinked, inhaling deeply as anxiety crept across her chest. Smiling, she said, "I'm handling it."

"I'm sure you are. You organized that gala three years ago single-handedly. The one at the Waldorf." She motioned as if to fan herself. "You were the envy of all that weekend, H."

"That was a long time ago."

She and Scarlett held each other's gazes. Eventually,

Scarlett said, "Well, I'm going to put some tea on. Then I'm going to spend the next hour convincing you to join me and George for dinner."

Chuckling, Harriet pulled the collar of her robe tighter. "You can try, Scar."

"Oh, I will." She grinned as she headed for the kitchen. Harriet watched her go, then refocused on one of the smaller headlines toward the bottom of the business page. It read: "Browning Lumber Mills Reach Record Low Production. Trouble Ahead?"

Carefully, Harriet clipped the article. She'd add it to the others before turning Scarlett down on her offer. She didn't have time for dinner out with friends. Not now. Maybe never again, she thought briefly with another glance at the Tiffany lamp.

A familiar hollow ache crept up her back. Before it could settle between her shoulders, she gathered the paper and stood. She was Harriet Browning, she reminded herself, heiress to the Browning timber fortune her father had spent his life building. She didn't have time for galas or dinners or larks out in the world she used to know. She had to focus. She had work to do.

CHAPTER THREE

A va frowned as she pulled the coffee cup and saucer toward her. The diner waitress had set it down in such a hurry that some of it had splashed out onto the table. She grabbed a napkin to dab at it, unable to keep from likening the dark liquid spreading across the table to the feeling of apprehension growing in her mind since leaving the postal annex the other day.

"JCPenney needs operator girls," Imogene said.

"I've seen those rooms. There's no windows, no air." Ava shook her head before taking a sip of her sugary coffee. "And those awful headsets."

"Fine. Moving on." Across from her, Imogene squinted at the want ads, her ham and cheese sandwich already gone. She took a drink from her Coke before saying, "Oh, the Eighth Street Theatre is hiring. They need ticket takers."

Ava considered it. "I do like the movies."

"I'll mark it. There's a dye factory in Queens." She frowned. "My grandma worked in one of those. I remember her skin always had a purple tint from being around the dyes all day."

In unison, they said, "Next."

Imogene studied the paper while Ava finished her tuna melt. She scooted her plastic chair closer to the table as a man in a large coat pushed by behind her. The diner was packed, its fluorescent lights gleaming over people on their lunch breaks. Bing Crosby crooned from a jukebox in the corner.

"Joe really doesn't mind if you work again?" Ava asked.

Imogene flattened the paper on their cluttered table, pushing aside the ketchup bottle. "He knows how much I like it. Besides, he's been away for so long, I think he enjoys being at home with Benjamin and Sally."

"You picked a good one."

Imogene smirked. "Don't I know it. Who knew that goofy football jock we met the summer before college would turn into such a great man?"

"Remember when we got a flat outside Pleasantville, nearly a mile from campus? He carried you back the whole way."

"I told him I wasn't a damsel in distress."

"Oh, he knew it. He was just too stubborn to let you break a sweat."

"Yeah, we saved that for later that night."

Ava laughed, tossing a crumpled napkin at her. Then they giggled at the incredulous look from an older woman at the next table.

"Those were the days," Imogene said, catching her breath.

A woman strode by, the clack of her heels catching Ava's ear. The way she stood at the counter, one hip out slightly, reminded Ava of another woman from another time. Before the memory could overwhelm her, though, she thumped the newspaper with two fingers. "Back to the matter at hand."

Imogene mimicked her movement. "I like the ticket taker notion."

"Won't be nearly as busy as the sorting room."

"What could be?" Imogene sighed. "That was one-of-a-kind."

Ava nodded. "I don't know. I want to find the right thing, you know?"

"That's respectable."

"Gee, thanks."

Smiling, Imogene said, "You've got time."

Ava snorted, putting down her coffee. "Tell that to my purse. And my landlord."

"How is Mr. Wakowski? I haven't been by in a while. I should bring over a tray of lemon bars."

Snapping her fingers, Ava said, "*That's* why he's been hounding me, the lack of lemon bars." She grinned. "He's the same. Old, demanding, in need of a bath."

"Good old Mr. Wakowski."

Ava drummed her fingers on the table, glancing at the date on the paper. April twenty-third. Three weeks since rent was due, and May the first loomed near.

"Mind sharing that lemon bar recipe with me? I'm only good for chocolate chip cookies."

Imogene straightened, putting on her hat after dabbing crumbs from her mouth. "Sure. I'll bring it by tomorrow."

"You're a lifesaver." Ava unclasped her green purse, but Imogene held up a hand.

"I got this."

"Imogene, I can still pay for lunch."

Her friend eyed her. "I really don't mind."

Ava pulled out eighty cents, leaving it on the table as she stood. "You can get tomorrow's. Same place, same time?"

Imogene smiled. "Wouldn't miss it."

As they waited for a cab outside, Ava chewed her lip. She shouldn't have insisted on paying. She needed every penny she had for rent. After seeing Imogene off, she laughed at the sudden empty feeling of her handbag. Her brother William always said she was too stubborn for her own good.

That night, there was a knock on Ava's door. Through the peephole, she found Mr. Wakowski. Rather, she found his round, wire-rimmed glasses plastered to the top of his forehead pressing against the door.

Putting on a smile, she cracked the door, leaving just enough space to peek through. "Good evening, Mr. Wakowski."

He shuffled as close as possible, his old loafers scraping the even older floorboards. Ava and Imogene had always joked that Mr. Wakowski had been born with the building. Both creaked with time and were in need of a fresh coat of paint.

"Miss Clark." Even his voice sounded worn. He dug through his trouser pockets, then searched inside his buttoned red sweater. Ava wondered what sort of pattern it might have featured once upon a time when he shoved a letter forward. "This arrived yesterday."

"Thank you."

He stared at her, his light brown eyes watery under a wrinkled forehead. Even in the dim hallway light, Ava could see the moles and sunspots dotting his vein-riddled hands and sallow cheeks.

She shifted, knowing he was going to ask about her unpaid rent this month. "I'll have it ready in two weeks, Mr. Wakowski. This month and next. I found a real promising lead today. A ticket taker at the pictures. Real promising," she added, making her smile so big it hurt.

He grunted. "You got till May third, Miss Clark."

"I understand."

When he left, she waited until his door down the hall closed. Shutting hers, she fell against it and exhaled.

She opened the letter on the fire escape, the warm air

lingering after the sun had set. Her father's straight stiff handwriting greeted her.

Hi, honey. Your mother and I know you must be busy. Paper keeps talking about a coal strike. Told your mother that's why we grow corn. People need corn. We'll be out in them fields if you come home. You know where to find us.

Ava could imagine her father laughing at his own jokes. She read the rest of the letter, then looked out at the towers of brick on all sides of her. A city of life and progress, filled with opportunities she'd dreamed of as a young girl.

She pictured her parents on their land—twelve acres of farm and home—in northeastern Pennsylvania. Her mother in her pale lavender dress hanging laundry on the line. Her father in his white shirt and suspenders, his back and arms strong as any machine he'd ever used to till the soil. She smiled at the memory of running between the waving stalks, chasing her brothers, whom she could never catch.

Ava sniffled, wiping a tear away. "No time for that," she said to the metal stairs snaking down her building. Back inside, she added the letter to the drawer where the others sat.

She reached for the stationery gathering dust but paused. Shaking her head, she retreated to the kitchen. Opening a can of soup, she reminded herself it was better if her parents thought her life was the way they imagined: busy, glamorous, and brimming with success.

It had been, at certain points. The last few years had found her the busiest she'd ever been. That was the way she liked it. But now...she glanced around, taking in her sparse, tiny apartment. Shouts came from upstairs. Dogs barked below. She was glad the war was over, but with its end so went her work. Not only that but any hope of finding her brother James fell into shadow with the items on her sorting room desk as they were boxed away.

She crossed her arms, leaning against the counter beside the stove as a warm breeze cut between the buildings and into her apartment. Admittedly, she was being picky about her next job, but the war-correspondence mail room had been everything. The energy, the enthusiasm of every single person working there had thrilled her. It had given her a purpose, a feeling like she was contributing. All of that was underlined by the far-flung hope that she might come across the one letter she'd secretly hoped to find. The letter that said her brother was no longer missing in action, that James was alive and coming home.

She let her arms fall to her sides and reached for the counter behind her, pressing her fingers into the cool surface. A memory drifted to the front of her mind. She was in another kitchen, this one decadent, with tall windows. Light filled the vast room. Harriet was pressed against her, her lips tracing up Ava's neck.

Back in the present, Ava turned around and, unsure what to do, turned the faucet on. She ran a hand under the cold tap, focusing on the feeling of the water over her fingers until the memory was once again locked away. A minute passed until she was certain her composure was regained. She turned the water off and dried her hands on a rag. A new determination filled her chest, and she turned to face the room.

"I'll look again tomorrow," she said to the lightbulb hanging from a chain over her kitchen table. "I'll find something. I know it."

CHAPTER FOUR

This time, when Harriet's phone rang on Tuesday morning, she found it quickly in the dark. "What?"

"Aren't you a ball o' sunshine?" Scarlett said.

"Sorry." Harriet sat up. "I didn't sleep well."

"I told you to take some of those barbiturates Martha's raving about."

"I think they may be why Martha is always raving about something," Harriet muttered. "Have you tried them?"

"Lord, no, honey. I'm not about to put that stuff in my system."

Harriet laughed. "But I should?"

"You're more…" The line was quiet as Scarlett seemed to consider her words. "Worked up."

"A Browning never gets worked up."

"I'm only saying. Why couldn't you sleep, anyhow?"

Harriet pushed off the sheets and comforter, sliding her feet into a pair of slippers. "My meeting with Father's advisors is at eleven."

"That's today? You ready?"

"I would have liked to have gotten more sleep. But, yes, of course." She switched on the lights. "I've got everything under control." She'd organized everything to the best of her ability, and though she was confident, a sense of unease kicked beneath each thought running through her mind. It hadn't helped that she'd dreamt of being locked inside her father's office, endless streams of legal documents slithering around her, constricting her until she couldn't breathe.

After promising to call Scar later and tell her all about the meeting, Harriet dressed and began to make sure everything was, in fact, under control. From nine to ten, she inspected every room, ensuring each one was clean and organized. She'd dusted the day before, careful that each wall painting, from her father's portrait in the library to the Rembrandts lining the hallway, was ready to greet guests.

Though she would host the meeting-goers in the living room, Harriet knew a place had to feel welcoming in every corner. "A person can sense if someone is hiding a pile of junk behind a closed door," her mother would always say.

All her life, Harriet had watched her parents' staff flit about the fifteen rooms of their Fifth Avenue penthouse. They had worked tirelessly to ensure the wooden floors shined, the furniture remained perfectly placed, and the ambiance always aligned precisely to whatever the occasion called for.

Only in the past five years—when Harriet had to let her family's staff go—did she begin to understand how much work went into maintaining the Browning estate. While certain tasks, like making beds and cooking meals, she actually enjoyed, other things were quite tiresome. Like dusting. God, Harriet had no idea how much dusting one had to do in a home this size. The first time she'd stood in the hallway—duster and rag in hand—she'd felt daunted by the sheer number of *things* to clean. Lately, though, she relished the time spent polishing and shining. It kept her busy. More so, it kept her mind busy.

At ten till eleven, Harriet was pulling back her long brown hair into a bun when the buzzer rang. She took one more look at herself in the baroque mirror above her vanity, itself littered with perfume bottles and jewelry boxes. The mascara made her blue eyes stand out. She opted for more blush than usual and a soft pink lipstick that complemented her fair skin and the bright florals on her floor-length dress.

She met them at the elevator. "Mr. Curtis, Mr. Gray, do come in." Both men were in their late sixties. The latter was six feet tall, while the former was shorter than her with heels on. Harriet took their hats and coats, hanging them in the gallery where she'd laid a tray of cucumber sandwiches. A pitcher of tea sat beside it. "How are you both?"

"My back aches, I can hardly see, and the doctor says my heart's 'in crisis.' You ever heard such a thing?" Mr. Curtis bellowed his remarks, more to Mr. Gray than to her.

"You've got to tell that cook of yours to hold off on the bacon, old man." Mr. Gray chortled, his long white beard shaking over his black suit. He patted Mr. Curtis's large belly, which struggled to be contained behind his vest and suit jacket.

"Balderdash. The doctor's a quack. I'm fit as a fiddle." Mr. Curtis grabbed three sandwiches as Harriet led them into the living room.

"Please, make yourselves comfortable," she said, and both men nodded before taking seats on opposite ends of the large leather sofa that took up a majority of the room. She'd opened the curtains, providing ample sunlight that made the wooden floors gleam around the edges of the expansive patterned rug. She took a seat opposite them in a blue wing-back chair with wooden arms engraved to look like lion heads, her father's touch.

Only when Mr. Curtis finished his sandwiches, licking his fingers, then dabbing his thin strands of black hair that streaked across his round head, did he meet Harriet's gaze.

"Well, Mrs. Atkins, as you know, we are here to discuss your father's portfolio."

Harriet crinkled her nose, forcing a smile. "Mr. Curtis, you'll kindly remember that I returned to my maiden name after my divorce. Miss Browning will do perfectly fine."

Mr. Curtis looked confused but carried on. "Very well. Miss Browning, we've finally had time to review certain aspects of his financial history, per your request. We've been quite busy. You no doubt have heard how we've been helping the Vanderbilts with their situation."

Harriet nodded. She'd read all about the downward spiral the family had found themselves in since the 1920s. Cornelius Vanderbilt's descendants hadn't possessed the aptitude for business, and the family's fortune had dissipated to a fraction of what it once was. The shift from rail travel to cars had expedited the downfall of their once-extravagant wealth. While Harriet was aware of the changing world, she struggled with dueling sentiments about such truths. She knew it was happening but hoped and prayed the change would somehow not affect the Browning name. The naivety of such thoughts, she knew, was silly. Yet this was the cycle of hope and denial she often found herself in.

"Well, it has come to our attention that your father made some, how shall we put this, peculiar investments before his death."

Harriet crossed her legs. "Yes. I know he put money into several entrepreneurs. He always liked to support young people."

"Yes, very good." Mr. Curtis shot Mr. Gray a look.

"Miss Browning, it seems your father also had money in the Bank of Trust."

"The Bank of Trust?" In her mind, Harriet ran through the

books in her office, her father's accounting books. "I've found no mention of that." A spike of panic filled her chest.

"It was done quietly. We knew he'd set some aside when you were a girl but couldn't remember where. We had to do quite a bit of digging. That's why we nearly missed it."

"But that was one of the banks that went under during the Depression."

"So they did."

Harriet worked to keep her back straight, but an uncomfortable tingling ran down her spine. "How much did he have in there?"

The men exchanged glances.

"How much?" The panic in her chest grew hot. The walls seemed to press inward, and she reminded herself to breathe.

"Well," Mr. Gray said, glancing at the framed Picasso in one corner of the room, then at the china cabinet packed with fine dishes. "The good news is, he took most of the money out before the crash. Unfortunately, he immediately invested it in another business that went under. He was always a confident man. He doubled down on his investment." Mr. Gray held her gaze. "In order to obtain the necessary funds, he took out a second mortgage on this apartment."

Harriet blinked. She laughed. "You must be mistaken. There's no such documentation of him ever doing that. My father wouldn't have done something like that without... without notifying my mother...or..." She trailed off. Swallowing, she said, "We would have known."

"Miss Browning—"

"There has to be a mistake."

Mr. Curtis frowned, his pudgy neck spilling out over his high collar. He reached into his suit jacket, then stood and handed Harriet a folded document.

An agreement with the bank and now defunct company held her father's wild, curling signature at the bottom. It was the same signature she'd seen on every paper in his office.

"What does this mean?" she asked, looking between them. "What does this mean, now?"

Mr. Gray cleared his throat. "Well, there has been a generous grace period from the bank since your father's passing. But that grace period ended three years ago, and now the taxes on this property need to be paid."

"I pay taxes. Every year, I—"

"The taxes accrued from the second mortgage, my dear. The bank is calling for their collection."

He handed her a second piece of paper. Harriet's heart pounded as she unfolded it. The sum stared back at her, and she felt faint. Mr. Gray's voice sounded distant when he spoke. "As you know, we had to close another of your father's mills upstate. It's projected two more in Washington will follow by summer. The simple fact is, the demand for lumber is dwindling. People want their offices made of steel, not wood."

Harriet felt sick. She clung to the papers, crinkling them in her tight grip. She bored her gaze into the cursive script that was her father's name. When she opened her mouth to speak, the same question came out. "What does this mean?"

"I'm afraid that, unless you can pay that sum before the end of September or come up with enough money to match the second mortgage, well…I recommend finding somebody to help sell this estate."

Harriet's focus snapped to Mr. Gray. "Sell?"

"You may want to consider consulting your former husband." Mr. Curtis glanced at a piece of paper he tugged from his pocket. "Mr. Lawrence Atkins. The bank may be willing to speak with him on this matter."

Harriet's disbelief shook into frustration. "Mr. Atkins does not live here. We divorced ten years ago. This is none of his concern."

"Sometimes, these things are best left to people more equipped to handle such situations."

"I am more than equipped to handle this." Harriet lowered her voice, not wanting to show her absolute fury at what was happening. "This is my home, Mr. Curtis."

Reaching one hand out, Mr. Gray said gently, "I know this is difficult, Miss Browning."

"This is my father's home. My parents, they…I grew up here."

"With respect, Miss Browning, were you not raised in Paris and occasionally London?"

She pursed her lips, staring at Mr. Curtis, who seemed to sweat under her gaze. "This is my home," she repeated. "You cannot ask me to sell."

Mr. Gray, looking worried, leaned forward. "Miss Browning, I have to recommend—"

"I respect your opinions, gentlemen. But you're wrong. This"—she held up the documents—"is a mistake. I'm going to look further into the matter. Things will sort themselves out, I assure you." She stood. "Now, I must insist you take your leave. I've much to do."

Quietly, the men gathered their things. At the elevator door, Mr. Gray turned. His tall figure stooped as he spoke low. "Miss Browning, please do see reason."

"I see perfectly fine, Mr. Gray. Thank you for your concern."

"We'll call again in a month," Mr. Curtis said. At her sharp glare, he hurried into the elevator.

"Good day, gentlemen." Once they were gone, Harriet let

her shoulders fall. She glanced again at the papers in her hand. The words seemed to swirl around each other. Confusion twisted in her mind until the image of her father formed. His proud figure shifted, grew smaller. This didn't add up. It didn't make sense. "Oh, Father. What did you do?"

CHAPTER FIVE

The following days found Harriet lost amid a sea of legal jargon and numbers that screamed at her from every corner of her office. Each new attempt to sort through her father's bank statements and business agreements led her back to the documents from Mr. Gray and Mr. Curtis. There was only one conclusion: the Brownings were in hot water.

"You really didn't know about this?" she asked her mother the next night over the kitchen telephone. Harriet clutched her glass of chardonnay like a lifeline as she listened.

"Your father was a busy man. You remember. The doors were closed to anyone who didn't have a beard or an Adam's apple."

"But you were his wife."

"And I was an excellent one. I made sure he was never disturbed. He took care of business, and I saw to our social affairs."

Sighing, Harriet took another drink, then switched the receiver to her other ear. There was a rustling, followed by a man's distant voice. The sound of clinking metal trailed after the heavy tread of someone's footsteps.

"Is Bud back from an afternoon ride?" she asked, not bothering to keep the sarcasm from her voice.

"As a matter of fact, he is. Had to help catch a couple of stray sheep with the neighbors."

"Mother. Do you hear the words you're saying?"

"What, dear?"

"Sheep are your neighbors."

"Oh, sweetheart. It's really not as rustic as you might imagine."

Harriet shook her head, staring at the remnants of wine at the bottom of her glass. She couldn't wrap her mind around the fact that her mother, Velma Browning—now Mrs. Thomas "Buck" Jackson—had left New York for a broad-shouldered, slow-talking ranch owner. Harriet never would have imagined her mother, "Miss New York City 1910" and the butterfly of any uptown gala, donning a wide-brimmed hat and chasing cows.

She must have sat in silence for too long when her mother said, "Come visit."

Harriet frowned, picturing the documents strewn over her desk. "I thought you were coming here."

"It'd be good for you to get away."

"Someone has to be here." *Somebody has to deal with all of this*, she almost said. Anger rose up in the back of her throat at her mother for moving across the country, leaving her behind after her father's death. But Harriet inhaled, quelling her irritation and biting back her words.

"You can't do all this alone, honey. Why don't you call Lawrence?"

"Not you, too, Mother."

"He has a head for these things."

"Why does everybody keep saying that?" She groaned. Though this time, she protested because her mother, like her father's advisors, were right. He *would* know what to do. They'd only been married a short time, but he had been incredibly capable of handling their finances, however briefly they'd been entangled. "Hold on." She set the phone down, annoyance fueling her steps to the office.

Harriet could handle this. She glanced again at the pile of folders and documents looming atop her desk. She fell back against the chair, scanning the large room that led to the rest of her life: her neglected letters to her father's mill managers, her sparse pantry, her cluttered bedroom floor. Perhaps if she did have someone to help with other things, daily tasks and chores, a butcher run, laundry, writing correspondence...that might be useful. Then she could focus on this mess.

Picking up the office phone, she said, "I don't need him, Mother."

"Darling, these are unusual circumstances. You're dealing with a stressful matter."

Harriet bit her tongue to keep from saying *And you're my mother. Why aren't you here?* "Maybe I can hire an assistant."

After saying something muffled on her end of the line, her mother replied, "Harriet, you can't really afford—"

"How much could they be, really?" She jotted down a note to peruse the want ads to gauge secretarial pay.

Her mother's voice turned serious. "You'd have to interview strangers, darling."

"Mother, how do you think Father hired our staff?"

"All of our people came highly recommended through the Carnegies."

"Well, the Carnegies would have a field day if they knew why I was looking for a personal secretary. I'll just place a vague ad where no one will see it."

It sounded like her mother was outside as a sound like a bell clanged. "Lovely, dear. And if you change your mind about visiting, the guest room is all ready for you. Buck will prepare his special chili."

Harriet swallowed the last of her wine, rolling her eyes. "Great. Good-bye, Mother."

She fell back in her chair, her arms listless at her sides. Her mother was right; she needed help. She mulled over various scenarios. She could hire someone for a few months. A young woman who could come by a few hours each day to keep the apartment in order while she made sense of the financial side of things. Somebody who could blend into the background. Yes, that was what she needed. A temporary, invisible assistant so that she could focus on what was important.

Harriet found that morning's newspaper, then switched on her desk lamp as the sun fell behind the building across the street. Begrudgingly, she folded open the social papers. Photos from an art exhibition at the Met exploded across the page. All of New York's elite had been there: the Astors, the Byrds, the Carnegies. Even Scarlett was in a photo with Dorothy Smith and Edith Post. Everyone wearing heaps of fine jewelry and dazzling smiles. Harriet couldn't remember the last time she had dressed up to go out. Last summer, maybe. Or was it the one before? She glanced again at the photos.

"My invitation must have gotten lost in the mail," she mused. Not that she would have gone, but it would be nice to know she was still welcome.

With a harrumph, she flipped to the want ads. Maybe she could post under a pseudonym. That way, nobody would know she was in need of assistance. Not that the Astors and Forbeses spent their mornings perusing this side of the paper. No, she was being ridiculous. She would be outright. Why not? She was already a social anomaly, the divorced heiress to a lumber fortune that was disappearing faster than she could fry an egg.

Glancing at the clock, she grabbed the phone again.

"Yes, Operator? Please connect me to Mr. Arthur Sulzberger. Tell him Harriet Browning is on the line."

❖

Ava's stomach rumbled as the waitress set a plate of sausage, eggs, and bacon on the next table. She glanced at her handbag next to her sweating water glass. The sad collection of coins and crumpled dollar bill within seemed to glare at her through the fabric.

"Just the toast for me," she said, handing the menu back to the waitress, an older woman with gray hair piled into a bun.

"I'll have the omelet with a side of bacon." Imogene smiled, then leaned forward when the waitress left. "You can have the bacon."

"You're the best." Ava rubbed the back of her neck, the leather strap of her watch grazing her flushed skin. Nearly a week had passed, and she still hadn't found the one, a job that really piqued her interest. A mild sense of desperation had crawled into her mind that morning when she'd drunk the last of her coffee and had to decide which to buy at the market: that or toilet paper.

It wasn't that she didn't have any money, but Ava needed to save everything she had earned from her last two paychecks to put toward rent. She wasn't frivolous, but everything she had ever earned went to her apartment and the bills that came with it. New York was great, but it was expensive.

"I have a feeling today's going to be the day," Imogene said as she adjusted the napkin holder in order to spread the paper out across the table.

Ava crossed her arms, glancing behind the diner counter and wondering if she'd be any good at making chocolate malts.

"Let's see." Imogene sipped her orange juice as more diners hurried through the east-facing door. The sunlit restaurant buzzed with early risers. She started to read aloud.

"Housework. Housework." She frowned, continuing, "Ladies 'young' for demonstrating and canvassing a necessity in life." She looked up. "What does that even mean?"

"Got me." Ava ran a finger around the rim of her glass, her stomach grumbling again, searching for food it hadn't had yet today. "Besides, I'm not exactly 'young.'"

"Oh, please. We're in our prime. Thirty-five is the new thirty." Imogene read off more items, mostly maids needed upstate.

Leaning to rest her forehead in her palms, Ava said, "I don't want to move out of the city for work, but it sounds like that may be the only option."

"Hold on. There's a few more. Let's see." Imogene puckered her lips as she traced her finger down the far-right column. "Oh, this looks interesting. 'Personal secretary needed for daily tasks. Manhattan.'"

Picking up her head, Ava said, "I'm listening."

Imogene continued. "It says, 'If interested, please bring personal references to 1030 Fifth Avenue to meet with Miss Har—'"

Ava straightened. The waitress slid their plates onto the table, but not even the scent of bacon broke Ava's gaze away from her friend's startled face. "What did you say?"

Imogene turned the paper over. "Nothing. It didn't sound that great after all. Maybe we'll have more luck tomorrow."

"Imogene."

Imogene pulled the newspaper closer, but Ava reached over her plate and tugged it out of her grasp. Her eyes swept over the page until she found the short, unassuming ad near the bottom.

She read, "...to meet with Miss Harriet Browning between 11 a.m. and 2 p.m. on Saturday May first." Ava stared at the name. The small, black print grew tall as memories broke through the diner wall, filling up the room until she was swallowed in hazy dreams. Harriet sat beside her on a picnic blanket on a clear spring day. Ava ran her fingers along the waist of Harriet's dress. The blue of Harriet's eyes shined as Ava leaned in close.

"Ava."

Snapping out of her thoughts, she met her friend's gaze. Momentarily, she felt lost, the lingering lake breeze pulling her into the past. Finding the edge of the diner table, she forced herself into the present. Taking a breath to collect herself, she asked, "Why would she need a personal secretary?"

Imogene shrugged. "She's bored? Why else do socialites do anything?"

Biting into her toast, Ava reread the ad. "She's offering fifty cents an hour."

"Because she has no idea that's more than most would offer. She never was grounded in reality, that one."

Ava frowned. Curiosity wandered out from the back of her mind and began to sing loud. It beckoned to her to learn more about what would drive the woman she hadn't seen since college to need help. The Harriet Browning she knew would never make such a public plea for assistance.

"Please tell me you're not seriously considering applying." Imogene's eyes were wide and concerned.

Ava tried to give an apathetic shrug. "What if I did?"

Imogene coughed on her juice, her eyebrows shooting skyward. She wiped flecks from her chin before leaning forward to practically hiss, "That woman"—she pointed at the paper in Ava's hand—"broke your heart into a million tiny pieces. I remember. I was there to sweep them up."

Ava grimaced, recalling the night she ran to Imogene's dorm room, flinging herself into her friend's arms hours before their commencement ceremony. Her body ached at the memory of what felt like years of endless sobbing only interrupted by dragging herself robotically across the ceremonial stage to receive her degree. Finally, she muttered, "I remember, too."

"Then how can you possibly want to see her again, let alone work for her?"

At this, Ava smiled, handing Imogene a napkin. "What if I don't go with intentions of working?" Imogene frowned as she dabbed her chin, but Ava pressed on. "What if I show up, wearing something fabulous, just to see what's going on? I mean, aren't you curious why she's placed this? And…" She shrugged, unable to keep the excitement from her voice. "I'll show her what she missed out on."

A faint smile lifted Imogene's lips, but only momentarily before her face fell serious again. "I don't know."

"Imogene, you and I both know I'm not the same person."

"Well, I suppose not."

A new confidence filled Ava. She bit her lip, tapping the newspaper. At Imogene's clouded gaze, she said, "Come on, it would be fun. No expectations. Just breeze in, breeze out."

Imogene sat back, crossing her arms. "Ava, you can't just breeze by Harriet Browning." Hesitating, she added, "You never could."

An old, nearly forgotten heat started up the back of Ava's neck. "I'm not a doe-eyed college girl anymore. She can't hypnotize me the way she once did."

For a moment, Imogene looked like she was about to respond. Ava could see the "How would you know?" batting around the air. And she had a point. It had been fifteen years since they'd spoken, let alone seen each other. But, she reminded herself, she wasn't the same person. She'd gone on clandestine dates in the city's underground nightlife—failed dates, but dates. She'd worked. Had experiences. She'd lived.

"I'm a different woman, Imogene," she said again, giving

her a wide smile as she bit into a piece of bacon. "I'm Ava Clark, former war-correspondence postal employee of the year."

After a moment, Imogene couldn't hide her grin. "That's right. You're capable of anything. You've got gumption now. And hootspa."

Ava laughed. "What is hootspa?"

"No idea. But you've got it."

Smiling, Ava said, "And I'm gonna show one Miss Harriet Browning all about it."

CHAPTER SIX

A va finally managed to push Imogene out of her apartment ten minutes before she had to leave to catch the train to Manhattan.

"The whole point is that I make an impeccable impression," Ava said. "You're going to make me late."

Imogene shot her arm back inside to scoop up her bright blue hat and handbag from the entryway table. The end of her matching knee-length dress caught on the splintered doorjamb. "Fine, I'm going." She pushed her face toward the shrinking space as Ava closed the door. "Are you sure you don't want me to come?"

"I'm sure. Thank you for the blouse and the lemon bars, but I've got to do this alone."

"Call me after," Imogene hollered before scurrying down the hall. "You still need to find a job, don't forget!"

Running into her tiny bathroom, Ava smoothed her hair behind her ear. Her blond locks had cooperated this morning, thankfully, falling in a gentle wave just past her shoulders. She ran a hand over her belt, then down her navy pants. Adjusting the collar of her salmon red blouse, she started to fasten the top button, then thought better of it.

She snatched her thin, worn leather watch from next to the faucet, checked her teeth for the fifth time, then grabbed her handbag back in the hall. "Can't forget these." She left the tray of lemon bars at Mr. Wakowski's door. With only two days before May third, she hoped this might help extend her rent deadline.

Only when Ava packed into the train headed for Midtown did she catch her breath. The glaring rumble of the car drowned out all thoughts save for those of where she was headed now.

Am I really doing this? She stared out the window, one hand holding the overhead bar as the train sped onward. *Of course*, she countered her own concerns. *Why not?* Harriet Browning had made her choice, and now Ava was going to show her just how wrong she'd been.

Several passengers over, a tall man in a tweed suit and fedora hummed an old song. Ava smiled as the familiar melody drifted over to her, beckoning old memories:

"Sorry, I thought this was the coat room." Ava paused, her jacket still over her arm as a lithe woman in a fine green dress and low heels turned to face her.

Ava was struck by the way the lamplight danced off this woman's blue eyes. She was also taken by her posture, which was impeccable, and how she seemed perfectly poised, with a nearly empty champagne glass in her right hand. A dark forest green polish to complement her dress was painted on her nails. She wore a thick gold bracelet on her right wrist.

"You're not wrong," the woman finally said, holding Ava's gaze. She gestured to a doorway to her right. "I'd gone to freshen up in the powder room, then found this." She nodded to a gold-framed painting Ava hadn't noticed. Though she was finding it difficult to look at anything but the striking woman before her, whose light brown hair was elegantly divided so that half of it was pulled back in a fine gold clip and the rest fell down her back in a gorgeous cascade. Worn like that,

Ava could study her round face, hosting a chin that seemed to always be slightly raised. Her voice pulled Ava's attention. "I absolutely adore his use of color."

Ava gave a small smile. She managed to find the chaise and dropped her jacket on top of a dozen others. When the woman turned back to the painting, Ava quickly smoothed her black skirt, then checked that the buttons on her blouse were aligned. She wasn't entirely sure why her throat felt suddenly dry. Attraction to women wasn't new for Ava, but she generally embraced those feelings with confidence. This time, an undercurrent of nerves carried her steps, but she swept those feelings aside as she moved across the room.

"He does seem to have a way with blending the reds and blues," she decided to say, standing next to the woman, who leaned closer to the oil painting, squinting a little.

"Yes. And this"—she pointed to what looked like trees or maybe buildings, Ava couldn't tell—"how he interprets the background, drawing our eye to the people by utilizing the horizon in such a way."

Ava stared at the woman's face in profile. She had a slender nose and an equally slender neck. The shine of a necklace that matched her bracelet glinted near the edge of her dress collar. She wore gold studs in her ears. Ava wondered if they were real. The way this woman carried herself, she thought they might be. Something about this woman, maybe it was the rapturous way in which she studied the painting or maybe it was the way she stood, like she belonged in this room and every other room she'd ever stood in. It drew Ava closer, beckoned her to want to know her better.

Clearing her throat, Ava said, "It's ever so important… utilizing the horizon properly." She licked her lips, then reached out, pretending to draw a line down the middle of the painting. "Imagine if it were vertical. God, what a disaster that would be. Those buildings over here would represent something else entirely." She waited. When the woman turned, she wore a surprised smile. Ava grinned. "They're not buildings, are they?"

"Trees." The woman laughed.

Dipping her chin, Ava said, "I spend most of my time in the science department."

"I was wondering why I'd never seen you before." Her gaze flickered down Ava's figure. "I would also wonder what you were doing at a Briarcliff art department social."

Ava shrugged. "I know people."

The woman arched an eyebrow. She stuck out her hand. "Now you know one more. I'm Harriet Browning."

Ava glanced down at her hand. She took it, surprised by the strong grip of Harriet's long fingers. "Ava Clark. It's a pleasure to meet you."

"You're a first year?" asked Harriet.

"I am."

"How wonderful. So am I."

"Are you from the area?"

Harriet's hand was still in Ava's, but at this, she pulled it back. Another surprised look graced her face. "You don't recognize my name?"

Ava frowned. "Should I?"

A small laugh escaped Harriet's perfect lips. "You must not be from New York."

"Pennsylvania."

"Well," Harriet said, "how about that?"

"How about that?" Ava echoed. She wasn't sure what the glint in Harriet's eyes meant, but Ava absolutely loved having it looking back at her. "Come on," she said, taking Harriet's hand. "Let me get you another drink." *As they crossed the room, she added over her shoulder, "You look thirsty."*

The train lurched, and Ava was thrown from her reverie, colliding with two men in long coats who were nose-deep in the morning paper. She glanced around. "Is this Lexington Avenue?"

"For the next five seconds it is."

She hurried out the train door and ran up the subway stairs into the harsh light of day. Ava scrambled onto the sidewalk and stood beneath a red awning outside a hardware store. Hundreds of people walked the only way she'd known New Yorkers to walk, quickly, with their heads down, as if every destination was the most important one, and they were half an hour late. Men with briefcases and stooping shoulders lumbered by while women cavorted along in fur coats, stylish hats, and long gloves, even though it was a fine spring day with only an occasional crisp wind cutting between the towering buildings. Even the breeze couldn't be heard over the cacophony of sound raging on all sides. Cars honking, vendors shouting on each corner, and people, people everywhere.

From her coat pocket—she'd opted for her finest magenta one, still several years old, that tapered at the waist—she pulled out the newspaper from the other day that Imogene had dropped off that morning. She knew the address, but the printed letters tucked beneath her arm reminded her this was real. Harriet Browning's address was in her hands for the first time in a long time. This was happening.

Taking a breath, Ava walked the rest of the way, twelve blocks, which felt longer than she remembered. When she found the towering apartment building on Fifth Avenue, she paused just beside the front entrance, far enough away so the doorman wouldn't think to open it for her.

"I'm really here."

It seemed the same. There were still bright flower arrangements in oversized pots framing the double doors.

There was still a young valet waiting at the curb. A well-dressed woman with a poodle in a large handbag walked by. Ava shook her head. She was definitely back. Years ago, this place had seemed magical, like a fairy tale castle. The glistening skyscrapers hosting glistening people were so shiny and new, unlike any world she'd ever been a part of. Now, the shine was still there, but Ava wasn't dazzled by it like she had once been. Instead, a soft glare bounced from the metal and towering windows. She held up a hand to shield her gaze.

Inside, she crossed the marble floor, its sandy color contrasting with the emerald wallpaper and gold accents. Plush chairs and gleaming tables were scattered throughout the vast first floor. The lobby was as she remembered it; only she didn't recognize the middle-age doorman at the base of the elevator.

"I have an interview with a Miss Browning," she said.

The man nodded. She caught his name printed on his nametag: Bert. "This way, Miss."

She followed him down a hallway that wrapped around the right side of the lobby, around the main elevator and stairs. Ava recognized it, too. It led to the private elevator to Harriet's apartment. Ava found their using it now peculiar. Why was Harriet meeting people this way? Why not greet them downstairs or in the lounge?

"Top floor."

"Yes." Ava realized it wasn't a question as Bert stood waiting in the elevator. She stepped inside, and he closed the gate. As it clanged shut, Ava's stomach kicked up in a flurry, trying, it seemed, to match the sudden jolt that came as the elevator leapt to life.

What if this was a mistake? What if Harriet took one look at her and laughed her all the way back to Brooklyn? Poor little Ava, still striving for things out of her reach.

The clang of the elevator chased her doubt away as they

rose higher. She took a deep breath. *No. I'm Ava Clark. I know exactly what I'm doing.* Was she curious about why Harriet needed a secretary? Sure. But she could quench her curiosity and keep her goal in mind. Harriet Browning had broken her heart once. Now it was Ava's turn to show her that there was nothing like a life of hard work to extinguish any ideas of love from her mind. Ava pulled back her shoulders. She'd show Harriet that marrying that ridiculous man had been the worst decision she could have made. No, leaving *her* was the worst decision Harriet had ever made.

Content in her decision, Ava smiled and stepped out of the elevator.

CHAPTER SEVEN

N ame?"
"Ava Clark."

The final line Harriet drew on her signature skewed off the page. She nearly knocked over her lamp before finding the woman she hadn't seen in more than a decade standing in her office doorway. "Ava."

The faintest smile graced Ava's lips, which were a captivating shade of pink that complemented her salmon blouse and navy pants. Her hair held a golden hue that made Harriet unsure where to look: the gorgeously arranged waves or Ava's light brown eyes that seemed to twinkle.

The smile faded, though, and Ava straightened. "Miss Browning, good morning. I recently read your ad in the paper for a personal secretary."

Miss Browning? Harriet replaced her pen and gathered her papers into a pile to give herself time to think. What was Ava doing here? She flicked her gaze across the room, replaying her words. "The ad?" she finally said.

Ava pulled a newspaper out from under her arm, giving it a wave. "That was you, wasn't it? Or am I in someone else's penthouse in the midst of what may be the most poorly executed robbery of the twentieth century?" She flashed a grin.

Harriet breathed a laugh but quickly composed herself.

She could feel her wits deserting her the longer Ava stood in her doorway. She cleared her throat, keeping her eyes down. "It was I who placed the ad." From the corner of her eye, she took in Ava's figure. The same worn leather watch sat at her left wrist. She seemed taller, though Harriet knew that wasn't possible. It was only the way Ava carried herself; her broad shoulders were pulled back confidently, not unlike when they'd first met. But unlike then, she now seemed to possess a grounded nature, giving off the sense that she was more self-assured than ever before. When Harriet's gaze climbed higher, she found Ava staring at her, one brow raised.

She strode into the office. "You're in need of a personal secretary?"

Harriet watched her as she stood at the window, pulling back the curtain the way she'd always done when she was here. It was so long ago, but Ava was back there, here, in her home. The gesture gave Harriet the oddest sense of déjà vu, like a ghost had wandered in as if it was the most natural thing in the world.

"I don't *need* one," she said, irked at the way her own voice pitched higher at the word need. "I simply imagined it would be useful to offer employment to somebody. It's been difficult for many since the war ended."

Ava turned, leaning casually with her back against the glass. "You're aware, of course, that the unemployment rate is declining?"

Harriet's jaw clenched. "Of course." She felt heat lick at the back of her neck. "I only wished to be of some help for… to the…"

"To the women who've lost their jobs since the men returned from overseas?" Ava asked.

Blinking, it took Harriet a moment to realize Ava was helping her. She wasn't sure whether to be offended or amazed that Ava could still read her so well. "Yes. Exactly. With the men back, all those hardworking women can't be expected to simply return home."

Ava smiled. "Not now that they've had a taste for work-life."

"Precisely."

Ava dropped the newspaper onto a side table. She glanced at the couch, and Harriet could see her consider sitting, but she seemed to think better of it.

"You are one of those women, then?" Harriet asked as Ava moved to stand near the fireplace; closer but still keeping a good distance between them. She raised one arm to lean against the mantel.

"What exactly would your personal secretary be required to do, Miss Browning?"

Harriet frowned at Ava's deflection. And what was with her insisted use of her last name? "The job requires being available from ten to six, Monday through Friday. They would assist with my correspondence, fetch groceries, and help keep this place in fine condition."

Ava glanced around. "Where's the other staff? I remember…" She cleared her throat. "I presumed there'd be others."

"I had to let them go."

"Oh." Ava placed her hands in her pockets. "It's only you, then?"

Harriet leaned back in her chair, aware of the shift in Ava's demeanor. Was that concern in her eyes? Ava had worn a similar look when she'd comforted Harriet at Briarcliff after a professor had rejected her art piece for the graduating class's auction. "Only me."

It seemed Ava had fallen into thought as she studied the ornate rug between them.

When she still hadn't said anything, Harriet stood. "Ava?" The sound of her name broke Ava's stare.

"The ad says you're offering fifty cents an hour."

"That's right."

"Will weekends ever be required?"

"I…no, I don't imagine."

"You're sure? No galas to help plan?"

Harriet flushed. "I haven't been to a gala in over a year." She didn't miss the surprise that crossed Ava's face, though she tempered it quickly.

She gestured to Harriet. "I don't understand, then. You seem perfectly capable, Miss Browning, of fetching your own groceries and writing your own correspondence." Her gaze hardened, an edge of slyness behind it. "Is this what New York's elite do now? Hire a personal pet to boss around?"

The sting of her words hit Harriet in her stomach. "That was fair," she said slowly. She leaned forward, pressing the pads of her fingers into the top of the desk. Harriet felt overwhelmed by the endless sea of scrutiny that waited outside her door, just below on the street outside her window. She could feel it. The gossip and the jeers lurked, waiting for her to step outside into their razor-clawed arms. But she couldn't tell Ava all of that. They weren't that person to each other. Not anymore.

Harriet took a long breath. "I have a lot on my plate, all right? My father is gone, my mother is riding cows in Nevada, and I'm here, divorced, alone, and with an inconceivable amount of work to sort through. My father, he—" She cut herself off. What was she saying? She straightened, aghast that she'd shared so much. And with Ava. She crossed her arms. "The woman I hire will be the only one who needs to concern herself with my affairs."

The soft, confused line between Ava's brow disappeared. "Very well."

Still feeling defensive, Harriet sat back down, pulling her chair tight against her desk. "If you have merely come here to prance around and gawk at the lonely heiress in her crumbling tower, then our time is done. You may see yourself out." She met Ava's startled gaze. "You know the way."

Ava's wide eyes gleamed. She took a breath; Harriet could see her chest rising and falling. She bit her cheek as a surge of emotions rose in her throat. "Very well. Good-bye, Miss Browning." Ava marched across the office. In the doorway she paused, one hand on the jamb as she said over her shoulder, "And good luck."

Harriet fell back in her chair, one hand on her chest, feeling as if the very air had followed Ava from the room.

CHAPTER EIGHT

Harriet felt like the dull tooth on one of the great automatic saws inside her father's mills. That feeling led her through the rest of the day in a gray haze, a bleary series of young ladies interviewing to be her personal secretary. Each of them fine candidates in their own right. Only one seemed dazzled by her and the elegant furnishings of her office. Harriet had kindly dismissed her, afraid she couldn't handle correspondence with the people Harriet knew.

For the others, it simply wasn't fair that Ava had thrown her shadow over their attempts to woo Harriet into employment. Two of the candidates seemed like excellent potentials, but as each of them spoke, all Harriet could hear was the *clack* of Ava's heels on the office's wood floor. She kept catching whiffs of Ava's perfume. And each time a new woman stood in the doorway, Harriet saw Ava there instead.

"Goddammit," she muttered at six o'clock while hunched over her desk. She stomped to the kitchen, poured a glass of chardonnay, then trudged back to the office. The cards of all the candidates lay before her, save for one. Ava had torn through like a breathtaking echo, reverberating off each corner of Harriet's home like a phantom, leaving nothing behind but her memory.

Harriet had pushed thoughts of Ava Clark to the back of her mind years ago. At first, after graduation from Briarcliff, she'd held them close. But they had been locked in a secret box, only opened on occasion through her short-lived marriage while she'd imagined it was Ava in her bed. After her divorce finalized only two years later, she had maintained a desperate hope that she might run into her somehow, somewhere. It was foolish, Harriet knew. Ava wasn't a part of New York's social elite. She'd always found the whole scene amusing. Harriet recalled the time Ava had struck up a conversation with Mrs. Byrd at a gala, never realizing she was speaking with the wife of a senator the entire time. Or if she had, she'd never let on. That had always been part of Ava's charm, her ability to slide right into any situation with ease and wit. "People are people, Harriet. We all want the same things at the end of the day. Doesn't matter how many diamonds are draped over their hands."

Harriet and Ava had wanted the same thing, once upon a time. But Harriet knew her girlish fantasy of a life with Ava was merely that, an unattainable whim. So the day she'd accepted Lawrence's proposal, she'd forced herself to move on. She'd thrown herself into painting, teas with Scarlett, and trips abroad. Soon, though, the dissolution of her marriage and then her parents' marriage had driven her back into this apartment. The tumult of that, followed by her father's death, had kept her focused, busy. The last thing she'd ever expected was to see Ava Clark again.

The fading sun cast an orange glow over her office. She took another drink, then walked over to the table where Ava had left the newspaper. Harriet picked it up, running her fingers along the edges. A small part of her hoped to find a number, a note, something to explain Ava's reappearance in her life.

"And what was with the Miss Browning?" she asked,

staring out the window at the street below. "You'd think we were strangers, not—" Harriet swallowed. Well, what were they, now? A sharp line of memory rose up behind her eyes. Ava's dorm room swam before her vision. There was shouting. Her head ached from crying. Ava slamming the door in her face.

"Focus, Harriet."

A long bath and another glass of wine helped soothe her nerves some. But that night, Harriet fell into dreams of Ava, of who they used to be before Harriet had ruined everything.

❖

Ava was certain she'd leave a jagged hole in the metal train car on her way home. It shocked her when the colorful advertisements taped between the windows remained intact, ignorant of the fury she felt vibrating off her like a rabid heat. Her rage at Harriet's entitled attitude fueled her steps along the crowded sidewalks after she stepped off the platform in Brooklyn. She stalked up the stairs of her building and sat with her jacket still on in her living room chair, staring at the wall.

"Who the hell does she think she is?" She gave a guttural hiss, throwing herself back against the dull plaid cushion. "She certainly won't keep anyone on for long with that demeanor."

A cold shower and a book only distracted her temporarily. She tossed and turned into the night. Throwing her arms over her head, she gave in and let her thoughts consume her mind. Fighting them was futile. Lying on her back, she released her musings and watched them sprawl out across the ceiling so she could better see.

She'd felt so confident when she'd first arrived at Harriet's. Even the smell of her penthouse was nearly the same: expensive potpourri and sandalwood candles.

She closed her eyes. So much had felt familiar. Even Harriet, but…Ava hadn't let herself even think about Harriet for twelve years. She hadn't realized until now that the Harriet she'd had to barricade from her mind in 1933 had remained the one she'd known then: college-aged, vibrant, and elegant. The Harriet she'd seen behind the obtrusive desk today looked rigid and…what was it Ava had seen in the corners of her blue eyes? A hollowness had tinged her gaze, lacing each word she spoke with an aching sadness.

Maybe Imogene was right, Ava thought, turning on her side. *What was I thinking? Did I even prove my point?*

"I have no idea." She sighed at the ceiling. She hadn't necessarily learned anything. She found she actually had more questions. When had Harriet's parents divorced? They'd never seemed particularly warm, but Ava remembered them being amicable toward one another. She recalled the image of Harriet slumped over her desk. What was consuming so much of her time that she needed to hire help?

Ava laughed. Harriet would never admit she needed anyone or anything. That hadn't changed. Still, it was clear she was losing a grip on things. Whatever those things might be.

In the dark and wrapped in her thin sheets as the foggy blare of cars continued by outside, Ava pulled her legs to her chest. A nearly forgotten part of her heart, the part with scars in Harriet's writing, cried out.

"Don't you dare," she muttered. "Don't you dare start feeling sorry for her."

Harriet Browning didn't deserve her sympathy. Not after what she had done.

CHAPTER NINE

The next morning at nine thirty, Ava scurried into the hallway in her striped robe. She intended to call Imogene to confirm their lunch date. Mr. Wakowski was coming up the stairwell, and she passed him on the way to the communal telephone at the end of the hall. His gray pants and faded white shirt seemed to blend into the wall.

"Good morning." She tried to sound cheerful despite the lack of coffee in her apartment and thus, her system, leaving her lethargic.

"Fourteen and a half hours, Miss Clark," was all he said before disappearing into his apartment.

"You're welcome for the lemon bars," she called after him. Right before she went to pick up the receiver from its stand, the phone rang.

"Hello?" She hoped it wasn't Mr. Wakowski's son. He was notorious for keeping whoever answered for at least twenty minutes before asking to speak with his father.

"Call from 1030 Fifth Avenue. Will you accept?"

Ava stared at the old wooden phone box on the wall. A flare went off in her chest as she said yes. Harriet's voice came through. "Ava?"

Closing her mouth, Ava checked that Mr. Alcala wasn't

peeking through his open door as she mustered her most indifferent tone and said, "Can I help you, Miss Browning?"

There was a sigh, followed by a sound like papers being shuffled. She pictured Harriet still behind that great desk, chained to whatever was troubling her. "Ava, please."

She swallowed, her tone coming out less stoic but still perturbed. "You called me."

"Right. I—" Another sound like the scratching of a pen on paper. "Ava, I think you'd be a good fit as my personal secretary."

"No one else applied for the gig?"

A snort from Harriet. Ava smiled as she listened. "Plenty of women applied. But you…" Ava pressed the receiver closer to her ear. "Well, you know this apartment. It's really as simple as that. I wouldn't have to train you on where things belong. It would save both of us a great deal of time." At Ava's silence, she repeated, "You know this place better than anyone else who applied."

I know you, too, Ava thought before pinching the bridge of her nose. God, what was she doing? She'd intended to sweep through in a dazzling whirl, leaving Harriet in a puddle of regret. She stared at the phone. Well, maybe she had. Why else would she call? She threw a glance to Mr. Wakowski's door.

"You sound confident," Ava said. "You mean to tell me nothing's changed in that mausoleum of yours?"

It was quiet a moment. "Well, the headboards in the guest rooms are new. Imported from Paris three years ago. There may be a new lamp, here or there." She cleared her throat. "My parents' belongings are generally gone. Otherwise, no, it hasn't changed much. But I…" Ava straightened, waiting as Harriet's words seemed to stick in the empty space between them. Eventually, she said, "Ava, I need your help."

She started to respond but was too startled by the confession. Harriet Browning didn't need anybody. That had been one of the first things Ava had learned at Briarcliff.

Harriet took a shaky breath on the other end of the line. "So what do you say?"

The image of a crystal blue lake swam before Ava's eyes. Their lake, she thought, smiling at old memories of their picnics next to campus. Ava saw herself standing at its edge now, her heart pounding in her ears. Harriet waited on the other side. She was too far away for Ava to make out her face. She stood at an angle. Was she turning to go? Or waiting for Ava to jump in?

This could only go one of two ways. First, and most likely, was the one where Ava dove headfirst, as she often did, into the water. She'd swim halfway across only for a sudden, sharp undertow to pull her down, leaving her in murky despair. It had happened before, so it was entirely possible again.

But a small part of her reached out, those jagged scars lining her heart coaxing her into an improbable hope. What if she made it across? What if she didn't drown in heartbreak? Even if it came to nothing more than a rekindled friendship, that could be something. She'd lost a lot over the past ten years. It would be nice to have something back.

Besides, she thought with another glance to Mr. Wakowski's door, she needed the money.

"It would only be temporary." Harriet's voice pulled her back to their conversation. "Only until I can sort things out."

"Only temporary."

"Once everything is settled, you'll be free to leave."

Ava bit her lip. Mr. Wakowski seemed to glare at her through his closed door, one hand out, waiting for her rent. "Fifty cents an hour?"

"Fifty cents an hour."

"No weekends?"

"No. Well, maybe one Saturday every now and then."

Ava took a long, deep breath. *Imogene is going to kill me.* "All right," she said. "When do I start?"

CHAPTER TEN

R ise and shine, darling."
Harriet rolled over, lifting her eye mask at the same time Scarlett turned on her bedside lamp. "What time is it?"

"Time for you to get dressed."

"Whatever for?"

"We're going out."

"Out?" Harriet propped herself up as Scarlett opened the curtains. Early morning light streamed in.

"Yes. I've got time before my calls later. I figured we could do Bergdorf's first. Then maybe JCPenney's."

"Scar," Harriet grumbled. "I'm not exactly in a place to spend my day shopping."

"I know that. But there is absolutely no burden on the purse by simply looking at a fabulous handbag through a window."

Harriet found her robe and went into the bathroom to wash her face. While she was confident in her ability to only window-shop, she was not secure in her ability to walk outside. She could see herself as if looking at her reflection in the shop glass, and shivered at the image. A once-prominent young woman with the world at her fingertips now keeping her collar high to avoid the gawking eyes of her former peers. She called, "I can't. Today's the first day for my personal secretary."

An audible gasp came from her bedroom. In the mirror, Harriet found Scarlett alight with glee in the doorway. "That's today? My, how time flies." Her impeccably made-up face fell. "H, you haven't told me a thing about this woman."

"Really, Scar."

"What? We're practically family. Truly, H. I'm offended."

"Offended because you won't be able to tell the ladies at tea later about my new hire?"

Scarlett lifted her nose. "Speaking of the ladies at tea..." She seemed to scrutinize Harriet, who dried her face, quickly brushed her long hair, then pulled it back into a tight bun. "A few of them are starting to say things. It isn't anything of substance, mind you. Not yet. But..."

"What, Scar? Spit it out."

"Well, darling, they say you're becoming a...a recluse."

Harriet barked a laugh. "Is that what they're saying?" She kept her eyes on the mirror. The confirmation of what she'd feared was happening, of what was being said about her, felt like the floor giving out beneath her. She focused on her reflection to keep steady.

"You don't come to the weekly teas anymore. You haven't in months. You're sequestering yourself from everyone."

"You're here."

"Only because the doorman loves me." Harriet finished pinning back her hair, then turned to face Scarlett, who said, "Dear, you can't stay in here forever under that ghastly pile of papers. You need fresh air. You're looking awfully pale."

"Thank you, Scar." She moved past her and headed down the hall. Scarlett followed. Harriet avoided her gaze, chewing her lip at Scarlett's news. Yes, Harriet hadn't called on anyone in some time. Each time she'd considered it over the past few months, something had pulled her back. At times, it was like the very furniture in this apartment gripped her, unwilling to let her go out into the world. A small part of her feared that it was actually she who clung to the confines of the walls. She wasn't sure what frightened her more: the world not wanting her anymore or her own self unwilling to want the world.

In the kitchen, Harriet put on water for coffee and found two eggs in the fridge. Scarlett eyed her, then dramatically fell on to the edge of the bench by the table. "What are you doing?"

"Keeping you company, of course. Really, H, has it been that long since you had a meal with anyone else?"

"You came over for lunch last week. Unannounced." She shot her a look. "I'm sensing a trend."

Scarlett waved a hand as Harriet let the eggs sizzle. "Maybe this secretary can get you to step outside once in a while." She tilted her head, putting on an innocent face. "What did you say her name was?"

Scooping her over-easy eggs onto a plate, she arched her brows at Scarlett. "Really now, it's nearly nine forty-five. She'll be here any minute." Setting the plate on the table, she pulled Scarlett from her seat, pushing her toward the elevator. *I need you gone before Ava shows up.* Harriet could only imagine the look on Scarlett's face if she knew who Harriet had hired.

"I thought she started at ten?"

"What if she's early?"

"What if she's late? You know, Martha Forbes gave me the name of her uncle's cousin's housekeeper. If this doesn't work out, I'd be happy to give you her information."

Harriet found Scarlett's handbag hanging on the coatrack. "Here. Now, please. I need to eat and get ready. I don't want—"

The elevator rumbled to a start. They both turned and watched as the thick black cable pulled the car higher. Harriet's throat went dry. She glanced at Scarlett. She hadn't wanted her friend here, especially not when Ava arrived. They'd never met, but Harriet had told Scarlett about her when she'd divorced Scarlett's brother. Scarlett had always known there had to have been a more significant reason for not staying married to her "dull but kind" sibling.

Now that reason was riding up the elevator.

Harriet helped pull open the gate, taking in Ava's dark pants, low heels, and white blouse. Her hair was half-pinned back and fell just past her shoulders in a gentle wave, the way it always did. "You're early."

"I caught the train at the right time. I hope you don't mind."

Harriet took her coat. Scarlett seemed amused, watching this exchange before stepping forward. "Now, H, you won't keep anyone around with that attitude. Good morning, I'm Scarlett. Scarlett Sachs, formerly Atkins."

Ava took her gloved hand. "How do you do? I'm Ava Clark."

Scarlett's brows shot skyward. Her gaze roved over Ava, then cut to Harriet above a sly grin. "Ava…Clark. Well, it is lovely to meet you."

Between Scarlett's tickled look and Ava's bemused grin, Harriet wondered if she'd fallen into a staged comedy. *God, this can't be happening.* Harriet practically shoved Scarlett into the elevator. "You'll be late, Scar, for that appointment."

Scarlett looked joyful. "If you say so." She waved to Ava. "I'll leave you to it."

When the elevator descended, Harriet let out a breath. She pulled the collar of her robe tighter and smoothed her hair. "Apologies. I didn't know she'd show up this morning."

Ava unpinned her hat. "That was Lawrence's sister."

Harriet blinked. "How did you—"

"I imagine there are only so many wealthy Southerners

with that name roaming the streets of New York." She flashed a smile, then pointed to Harriet's bare feet. "Did you just wake up?"

"I was making breakfast."

Ava nodded. She shuffled to one side, and they stood awkwardly across from one another. "Oh," she said, reaching into the coat she'd hung up. "I took the liberty of bringing your paper up. Figured I could save Bert the trouble." She handed it over. "He said you like the business papers on top."

"So I do." Harriet smiled. "Have you eaten?"

Ava looked thoughtful before she shrugged. "Got any coffee?"

"It should be ready. Come on. I'll show you where to start." A flutter turned in Harriet's stomach, but she reminded herself that was simply old emotions playing out of habit. A reflex, she told herself, at Ava's presence. This was nothing like before. This was professional.

❖

After drying their coffee mugs—which were finer than any collection of dishes Ava had ever owned—and gobbling a pear with some cheese, Ava headed down the hallway. Harriet had scarfed down some eggs and retreated to her office to start work. The carpeted hallway was dark, made more so by the three closed doors lining the right-hand side. She was about to join Harriet when she paused at the last guest room door.

"If I remember right, this one..." She opened it. "Yes. The sailing room. How could I forget?" She smiled at the bombardment of blue that leapt off the queen-size bed, the wallpaper, even the carpet. Each built-in shelf on the opposite wall above a desk was lined with nautical accoutrement.

Sailing instruments, jars of seashells, sea-themed books, and those tiny ships in glass bottles all lived here, stranded ashore in upper Manhattan.

Ava crossed the room to open a window. "It's not a sea breeze, but fresh air will do this room some good." She ran a finger along the edge of the desk, the same one she used to study at the summer she'd spent six weeks here. This room, the entire penthouse really, had seemed to trill with life. Now, it was as if she could hear the very sands of time gathering upon the windowsills.

She backtracked down the hall, curiosity getting the better of her. She opened the next room's window, then lingered in the third room back near the kitchen. It was the largest of the three guest rooms. Ava did a turn, wondering if she was, in fact, in the room she thought. The floral wallpaper she remembered had been replaced by a more neutral, plain eggshell. The walls still boasted framed art, and several finished canvases stuck out from beneath a large sheet in one corner next to a vacant easel. The large case hosting Harriet's art supplies—to Ava's surprise—was gathering dust beneath an old but beautifully lavish desk in the opposite corner. Fifteen years ago, this room, like all the others, had felt vibrant in every sense. She could smell the oil paints mingling with the scent of Harriet's perfume. She could feel the breeze through the window that had always been open while Harriet painted, and Ava—tired from studying in the next room—came to watch her work.

Ava moved to stand at the foot of the bed. Though the duvet was different, a pale gray to match the other muted tones the room had taken on, she knew it was the same one. She grazed the comforter with her fingertips as her gaze fell to the pillows. Like mist rolling in from the harbor, two figures appeared, wrapped in each other's arms and tangled in the sheets. Harriet had her finger pressed to Ava's lips, urging her to keep quiet.

Inhaling sharply, Ava hurried from the room.

In the office, she found Harriet had dressed. She wore a cream-colored dress with pearls in her ears to match. The few stray hairs Ava had noticed when she'd arrived were now diligently pulled back into an airtight bun.

"I opened some windows in the guest rooms."

Harriet didn't look up from what appeared to be an accounting ledger. "Thank you. Do you mind?" She gestured toward a table near the sofa. "There's some correspondence I've been neglecting. Can you organize it by date and sender?"

"If it's from the Byrds, keep it at the back?" Ava asked, grabbing the tall stack of unopened envelopes, each with curled script across the front.

Harriet smiled. "They do remain utterly insufferable."

Ava laughed. For a moment, it felt as if she was back in that summer. Memories mixed with the present, and Ava cleared her throat as she shuffled through the envelopes, though she wasn't reading the names. An odd sense of melancholy climbed across her shoulders. So many wonderful times here had been tainted by how things had ended. Being here, laughing once again with Harriet…how was Ava supposed to feel about that?

She was about to sit when a wooden box caught her eye. It was settled between two rows of leather-bound books, which all the shelves in the grand office boasted. Lifting the lid, she was hit with the old familiar smell of Mr. Browning's cigars. "This entire room smelled like these," she said, running her fingers over the lines of fine Cubans. In the lid, a polished silver lighter sat in a pouch. "Each time I was here, your father was smoking one of these. And so were each of the men he was meeting with." She turned and could practically see the clouds of gray billowing over even grayer heads. "He sat right behind that desk. The way you are now."

Harriet paused in her writing. After a moment, she looked up but only to scan the office. Her gaze flickered from the sofa to her desk, then to the window. When she did meet Ava's gaze, she said, "Close that, please."

Ava did so. She knew Mr. Browning had passed away years ago. She'd only known, though, because one of the supervisors in her office had a newspaper open as she'd brought him his coffee. There on the front page she'd read, "C.M. BROWNING, LUMBER KING, DEAD." She'd stared at the print, bombarded for the first time in a long time with the knowledge of the Brownings' existence. Well, now with the exception of Charles Browning, the lumber king.

Ava hadn't called or written. She couldn't. Any restringing of the lines that had tied her and Harriet together couldn't be touched. Ava couldn't go there again. Yet here she was now. Standing in Charles M. Browning's office, across from his daughter, the woman who'd broken her heart.

Snap out of it. Do what you're here to do.

Taking a seat, Ava glanced again at Harriet. She wore a serious expression, her head resting against her knuckles as she wrote. Sifting through the letters, Ava used the coffee table in front of her to make separate piles. After a few minutes, she sat back, frowning.

Nearly every letter, save for one from Harriet's mother, was dated March. Early March, at that. More than half hadn't been touched for over a month. Was Harriet deliberately ignoring her mail? If so, why?

Ava leaned forward to rest her elbows on her knees. She pretended to rearrange the letters but studied Harriet.

Closed windows. Private interviews. And whatever she was working on over there.

Ava didn't care about Harriet's affairs. She hadn't cared about them in fifteen years. This entire endeavor was about quelling her curiosity. And paying rent. Yes, Ava told herself, curiosity was the feeling that had sparked to life the moment she'd returned to this apartment. And it was curiosity that drove her thoughts now. Thoughts like, what in the world was happening to Harriet Browning?

CHAPTER ELEVEN

Harriet added the closing sentence on her letter to the bank. She reread the page, the end of her pen between her teeth. It had to be perfect; she couldn't afford to let on that she had little idea what she was doing.

A faint growling noise made her look up. She was surprised to find Ava sitting on the leather sofa. Harriet blinked, reminding herself that she'd hired Ava. Of course she would be in her apartment. Still, the visual was taking some getting used to.

"Sorry." Ava clutched her midsection. "Guess I'm hungry."

Harriet sat back, glancing at the desk clock. "It is nearly one." She noticed the two dozen small piles in even rows across the coffee table. Ava sat back on the couch, a pleased but curious look on her face. "That's very organized."

"It's one of my strong points."

Harriet smiled. "If I recall, you once arranged my paints by color and name."

"Someone had to. Leaving them scattered all willy-nilly with the reds and whites mingling was asking for trouble." She flicked her gaze to Harriet, then refocused on the letters. "You said whoever is hired on will be informed"—she nodded to the desk—"regarding what you're working on over there." She hesitated before adding, "And your family's finances."

Harriet set her pen down. "So I did." Standing, she motioned for Ava to follow. "Come on, I'll explain things over lunch."

In the kitchen, they sat across from one another at the table.

"So your father made some bad investments?" Ava shrugged, finishing the last of her cucumber sandwich, then downing a glass of milk. Harriet decided not to comment on how quickly she'd cleaned her plate. "You have funds, don't you?"

Harriet blotted the edge of her mouth, her gaze lowered. "Well, Father's mills have been closing, slowly but surely, over the last ten years. The need for timber isn't what it once was." Glancing up, she found Ava turning her empty glass, her gaze thoughtful. Harriet smiled at the familiar gesture.

"The wars did demand metal."

"Yes. The world in general seems to be shifting to one of concrete and steel." Harriet gestured to the corner window and the buildings beyond.

Ava nodded. "The funds aren't great, then?"

Harriet chewed on her apple slice. She'd left out the part about her father putting the apartment up as collateral after investing in a failed company. It was too awful. Harriet struggled to believe it, despite staring at the numbers all day and to her dismay, dreaming about them at night. She couldn't bring herself to admit to Ava that she might be losing her home in a matter of months. "Not great," she finally said.

"And your mother isn't helping? She's really herding cattle in Arizona?"

"Nevada." Harriet laughed. "I know. It's hard to imagine." She let her laughter linger, hoping it covered the low-lying resentment in her throat. Harriet loved her mother, but part of her was angry at her running off to the other side of the country, leaving Harriet alone to handle this.

Ava leaned back, crossing her arms. Harriet swallowed as she noticed the open top button of Ava's blouse that revealed the hollow of her neck. Old, intimate memories bombarded her thoughts, and she closed her eyes briefly to force them away when Ava said, "Velma Browning, the queen of couture, living in a barren desert."

Harriet shook her head. "I never would have thought it possible."

"I guess people can surprise you."

Harriet cut her gaze to Ava, who seemed to realize what she'd said. She stood quickly, taking both their plates. At the sink, her back to Harriet, she said, "What do you need to do to sort things out?"

"Well," Harriet said with a sigh, "since it's just me, I've been meeting with Father's advisors monthly. I want to believe their numbers can't possibly be right." At Ava's incredulous look thrown over her shoulder, she added, "I know. Numbers aren't my strong suit, but…" It can't be true, she thought, digging a finger into the table's surface.

"You'll figure it out."

Harriet stared. Ava still had her back to her, drying their glasses. Such a simple phrase. A single encouraging sentiment. Yet it was something Harriet hadn't heard from anyone since discovering her family's financial woes. A thin sliver of something new cut through Harriet's chest. It let in the faintest sense of hope while simultaneously releasing some of the pressure that had piled itself onto her shoulders.

Ava hung the rag above the sink, then turned to lean against it, meeting Harriet's gaze. Harriet nearly said, "It's so nice having you here," but bit her tongue. She couldn't afford to lose herself in distraction. She'd weighed the pros and cons of hiring Ava. She hadn't been sure Ava would even consider it, but everything she'd said on the phone had been true: Ava knew this place well, and even though it had been a long time, Ava understood her, too.

Granted, she wasn't the same person, but something told her to ask Ava to work for her. Even that morsel of belief just now had shined like a beacon of light in Harriet's dark world. That was worth whatever baggage they clung to in the meantime.

Harriet tore her gaze away. "There's much to be done." She found a paper under a year-old department store catalogue. "Here's the grocery list I made last night. They know what I like." She held the paper out. Ava looked at it, then her. Harriet sensed a question, but Ava only took the list. "Tell them to put it on my tab." Then she headed back to her office, closing the door behind her.

Her back pressed against the door, safely on the other side, Harriet exhaled. It would be a balancing act, juggling this newfound hope from Ava's presence with the reality of her situation. But that was fine, she could handle it. She only had to keep the image of Ava in that blouse, standing in her kitchen, deep in the corners of her mind.

❖

On Friday night, Imogene came over to Ava's apartment for dinner: half a roast chicken with lemon sauce, grilled asparagus, and a bottle of red wine, all compliments of Harriet.

"She's paying you fifty cents an hour *and* giving away full meals?" Imogene asked after Ava poured her a mug of wine.

"Perks of the job," Ava said, clinking their cups together. "Turns out she's become a good cook."

"Is this the only perk?" She raised a suggestive brow as she took a sip.

"Imogene!" Ava was glad her face didn't warm despite the flip her stomach did at such a suggestion.

Imogene bit the end of an asparagus, chewing as she replied, "It's a valid question."

Ava laughed, shaking her head. "I must admit, I was nervous at first about how it would be, working in the same space as her. But after a week, I gotta say, it's not bad."

"It still seems odd." Imogene leaned back, pushing her plate forward. "She makes you fetch her groceries? Deliver her laundry?"

"She's paying me to do those things."

"Is she injured?"

"No."

"Ill?"

"I don't think so." At Imogene's skeptical frown, Ava shrugged. "She's really busy. Apparently, her father left a bit of a financial mess after his death."

Imogene's eyes widened. She leaned forward. "Really? Is it like what the papers said about the Vanderbilts?"

Ava took a long drink. She shouldn't have said that. It was Harriet's business, and she was Harriet's employee. The helpless look she had seen in Harriet's eyes the last week when she'd seemed to float adrift behind her father's desk, filled Ava with the strange urge to protect Harriet's reputation. Of course, this only muddled Ava's thoughts even more. "How's Joe? And the kids?"

Imogene squinted at her change of subject but sat back, taking another bite of chicken. "You're right. It's not my business." She waved a hand. "They're fine." She glanced at her watch. "I need to be back in an hour. He's got his bowling league tonight. Oh, you'll never guess what Benjamin did this morning. I didn't know a six-year-old could make such a noise."

For the next half hour, Ava listened to tales of Imogene's children that reminded her she was glad not to have any. "I don't know how you do it," she said, clearing their plates.

"It's been easier while I'm between jobs. I can help. I did run into Mr. Barkley from the postal annex the other day, and he told me about an office that needs stenographers."

"That course you took will finally come in handy."

Imogene laughed. "My thoughts exactly. Oh." She dug into the front pockets of her polka-dotted dress. "That reminds me. When I saw him, he had a letter, said he was on his way to send it, but I told him I could deliver it." She stood and set the letter on the counter next to Ava, who scrubbed lemon sauce off their plates. The address of the military's northern post in London was written in block print. Gently, Imogene said, "I didn't know you'd sent another one."

Ava stared at the envelope. She dried her hands, then turned it over carefully. "I sent it four days before we closed." She'd mailed similar letters over the past three years, all to different outposts across England, all places that might have known where her brother had been since he disappeared. She looked up to find Imogene wearing a sad but encouraging smile.

Ava opened the letter. After a moment, she read, "We regret to inform you that the whereabouts of Private James Henry Clark remain unknown, despite all previous efforts to locate him. He remains classified as Missing in Action as of May 1944."

Imogene reached out, squeezing her arm. "I'm sorry, Ava."

She shrugged, swallowing a sob that crept up her throat. "Lots of soldiers weren't found. It doesn't mean he's not out there, somewhere." Crossing the room, she opened her table drawer. Next to her parents' letters were the other ones sent from the government, including the one her parents had mailed to her after William had died. She clenched her jaw. At least with William, she knew. These letters about James, she hated. They teased her, taunted her. Yet she couldn't stop sending inquiries. James wasn't dead. Missing wasn't dead, she'd told herself for the last four years. Though she knew the odds were slim, until it was as plain as watching William's coffin lowered into the ground, she couldn't bear to be the only one left. She couldn't bear to think that after they all got out of Pennsylvania, she was the only Clark left standing.

Closing the drawer, she turned. "Thank you, Imogene. For being here."

Imogene had gathered her hat and coat. She smiled. "Thanks for dinner."

At the door, Ava said, "Tell Joe hi, and give the kids a hug from me."

"I will." Imogene paused in the open doorway. "Be careful."

Ava knew she meant Harriet. "She's different, Imogene."

"Time plays tricks. It gives us a real nice pair of rose-colored glasses."

Ava smiled. "Good thing I have perfect vision. Don't worry so much, okay?"

"It's my nature. I was born worried."

Laughing, Ava replied, "Trust me. Me and Miss Browning? It's all business."

After saying good-bye to Imogene, Ava flopped into the recliner. Amid the dozens of compartments she'd built in her mind, labeled things like "Rent Money" and "Unanswered Letters," a new one sprang up. No. It wasn't new. Simply pushed aside, shoved toward the back, forbidden from being touched for more than a decade. She pulled it to the front, though, finding a new need for the one marked "Harriet Browning." The need to make sure the box remained unopened. The need to keep Harriet at arm's length. Her own voice echoed around her. *It's all business.* She reached out as if to trace her fingers over the lid kept firmly shut on what she and Harriet had once been. All business, Ava told herself again before forcing the old box of memories back into the recesses of her mind.

CHAPTER TWELVE

There's no new information? Nothing that can help me?"
Harriet pursed her lips, frustration threatening to draw
them into a scowl.

Mr. Curtis finished his brandy in her office. "I'm afraid
not, Miss Browning. If you like, I can call Mr. Atkins. I'm
sure he—"

"I've told you, that's not necessary." At her raised tone,
both men set their glasses down, exchanging looks. *Calm
yourself.* "Gentlemen, thank you, but I'm handling it."

"The bank is giving you until the end of September," Mr.
Gray said. "Your father was an upstanding, hardworking man.
He did a lot for New York. For this country. It's a generous
timeline."

"The wars were the best thing that could have happened
in your case," added Mr. Curtis. Harriet turned, noting that
Mr. Gray's open mouth matched hers at such a comment.
"The world was at war. There was hardly time to attend things
such as accrued debts. It's the same for many others like you,
Miss Browning. Everything was set aside while we fought
overseas."

Harriet nodded. "I see."

Mr. Gray cleared his throat. "Either they receive equal

payment by the end of September or…" He glanced around the office. "It will be a pity to see this place go."

"I have no intention of letting that happen." Harriet stood, the men following suit. *Even if I have to start selling Grandmother's china.* "Thank you for your time."

"We'll be back the second week of June." Mr. Gray gave a slight bow. Mr. Curtis was already pushing open the office door. "Good evening, Miss Browning."

Once they'd gone, Harriet flopped onto the sofa, staring at their empty glasses, the lamplight making the crystal shine.

Faint footsteps made her sit up.

"Just me," Ava said, a glass of white wine in her hand.

Harriet adjusted her hair, suddenly aware of how wrinkled her black skirt was after a long day. "I thought you'd be gone." She looked at the wall clock. "It's after seven."

"Well," said Ava, taking a seat at the other end of the sofa after handing Harriet the wine, "a meeting behind closed doors usually means stress. Given your circumstances, I didn't imagine Mr. Gray and Mr. Curtis came bearing good news."

Harriet took a sip, relishing the wine as it slid down her throat, warming her chest. She smiled, propping her right arm on to the edge of the sofa. That sliver of hope in her chest widened, seeming to grow at Ava's thoughtful gesture.

Ava shifted to face her. "What?"

Lifting the glass, she said, "You remembered."

"That you have more chardonnay than blood in your veins?" Ava replied. "Hard to forget when one of New York's elite drinks her entire art class under the table."

Laughing, Harriet said, "I'd forgotten about that." They shared a smile. "It wasn't a great meeting tonight. But I'm hopeful things will work out."

They sat quietly for a moment. Harriet relaxed as the wine dulled the stress of the last two hours. She studied Ava, who fiddled with the end of her blouse sleeve. The shirt was paired with a fetching pair of wide-leg slacks and low heels. Her blond hair had been pulled back in a lovely low underpin. The style always reminded Harriet of a tranquil, pastoral painting, and a flash of Ava in a prairie dress on her family's farm ran through her mind.

"I've been completely rude," she said after a minute.

Ava frowned. "I'm sorry?"

"You've been working here for three weeks, and I haven't asked after your family once. Tell me, how are your parents?"

Ava's gaze cut to the rug. "They're well. Still on the farm."

"Have you been back to visit?"

"Not lately. Work kept me busy." At Harriet's silence, she added, "I was a mail filing clerk during the war."

"Really? How was that?"

Ava gave half a smile. "I loved it. It felt essential, helping letters and telegrams make it to their destinations." Her face fell, and Harriet wondered at the sudden darkness in her eyes. "The war created so much chaos, so much uncertainty. The mailroom acted as a sort of safe harbor. Despite the bloodshed and mayhem happening across the ocean, those letters provided a lifeline. Gave people hope."

Harriet shifted, confused by the sudden urge to reach out. She took another drink to give herself something to do. "That's lovely."

"It was good work."

The tension made Harriet want to fill the silence. "And your brothers? How are they?" She smiled at the memory of meeting Ava's middle brother when he'd visited the city one summer between semesters.

The darkness spread over Ava's face, though she blinked rapidly as if to disperse it. "William died eight years ago."

The warmth in Harriet's chest turned cold. She set her glass on the coffee table. "Oh, Ava. I'm so sorry."

"He was part of Operation Compass in Egypt." She gave a sad laugh. "I didn't even know war had touched that part of the world." Shaking her head, she added, "I didn't know a lot."

Hands in her lap, Harriet asked, "Is that what prompted your job decision?"

"Yes. I wanted to learn more, to be of help somehow. The factories were full, already brimming with braver women than me building bombs and planes. Imogene's husband had connections, and we both got jobs in the filing office in the West Side, off 57th Street."

You've been here all this time? Harriet couldn't believe how close they'd been without knowing it. She shifted nearer on the sofa. "And James?"

Ava gave an audible swallow. "He was stationed on the southern coast, near Slapton Sands, two months before Normandy. The Germans had gained intelligence of a rehearsal for that very event, Exercise Tiger. Two tank-landing ships were preparing a run-through when they were hit by enemy torpedoes. Some of the men succumbed to burns and blast injuries. Others drowned and some…" Her voice trailed off. She cleared her throat. "They said James was on one of the ships, but he was never recovered. He was officially declared missing in action in May of 1944."

"My God." Reaching out, Harriet rested a hand on Ava's knee. Her face, which had been a mask of pain, grew blank, the lines on her forehead smoothing. The tense line of her jaw relaxed.

After a moment, Ava pulled back her leg, shifting away. "The war was hard for many."

"Ava." This was another of the changes Harriet had noticed

since their reunion. In college, Ava had been lively, open. She'd shared everything. Harriet understood why she would be closed off to her now, but the solemn air that sometimes engulfed Ava made Harriet tremble. She could only imagine the pain Ava must have been in since losing her brothers. She swallowed, trying to think of something else to say.

"He may still be out there. He's a strong swimmer. And knowing James, he probably missed call that morning and was stumbling out of a pub from the night before. He's probably shacked up with a British gal somewhere." She spoke to the desk across the room. "Missing isn't dead. James could still be out there."

Harriet started to speak, but decided against it. She knew the grim reality of what MIA meant. And Ava didn't look ready to accept that for her brother. Not yet. "I'm sorry, Ava." Wiping her eyes, Ava shrugged again. When she laughed, Harriet asked, "What's so funny?"

"I came in here because you were the one in need of a drink."

Harriet smiled. "Let me get you something."

"No." Ava stood. "Thank you, but I'm all right."

Harriet was at the drinks cart by the bookshelves. "Are you sure?"

"I ought to be going anyway."

A strange pang struck below Harriet's ribs as Ava started for the office door. "It's, um, getting late. You could...you could stay." At Ava's surprised look, she added, "The guest room's yours if you like."

Ava shook her head, and Harriet yearned to know what the hint of a smile meant as it lifted her lips. "My landlord will think I've fled if I'm not there when he lurks down the hall in the morning, and I didn't leave my lights on. But thanks."

Harriet nodded, still at the drinks cart. She felt oddly silly and pretended to rearrange the liquor decanters when Ava called, "Good night, Miss Browning."

She caught Ava's wink before she retreated down the hall. The tightrope Harriet had been walking since employing Ava gave beneath her, and she felt as if she was toppling over. Quickly, she poured a drink, letting the liquor burn her throat and quash the urge to call after Ava. She took a deep breath. Familiar feelings gathered around, threatening to unravel her, knock her sideways. She couldn't afford such a setback. She replaced the glass, brushed a hand over her hair, and returned to her desk.

Chapter Thirteen

A batch of lemon bars, plus last and this month's rent." Ava handed the plate topped with an envelope full of cash over to Mr. Wakowski. His eyes bulged behind his glasses. "Have a wonderful day," she added, then threw her jacket over her shoulder and strolled downstairs.

Outside, she breathed in the city. More than a month of employment with Harriet and things were going well, much to Ava's astonishment. They were getting along swimmingly. Harriet was busy most of the day, hunched over her desk, poring over those numbers like they'd change if she stared long enough. Ava, meanwhile, ran to the butcher, the grocer, the dry cleaners, and kept Harriet's apartment in order. It wasn't hard with only Harriet living there and keeping to her room and the office.

"Good morning, Bert," she called, crossing the immaculate lobby.

He tipped his hat. "Good morning, Miss Clark. Here's today's." He handed her the paper, and she gave him a coffee she'd picked up from the corner cart. It had been their routine for the last week since Ava had a little extra change leftover from her pay. He'd refused to accept her offer the first day, but after her insistence, he'd smiled sheepishly and thanked her.

Upstairs, she wandered into the office. "Miss Browning."

Harriet looked up. Her hair was in its usual bun, pulled so tight, Ava always wondered how it could be comfortable. Her blue eyes looked cloudy, as if she was half-dazed. "Oh, is it ten o'clock already?"

Ava eyed her wrinkled sweater, wondering if it was the same one she'd seen on Friday. "It is. Can I make you coffee?"

Harriet waved her pen. "I've had plenty, but do help yourself."

Next to the sofa, Ava turned when the lamp on the side table caught her eye. "Where's the Tiffany?" she asked, pointing to the silver modern lamp she recognized from the dining room.

Harriet kept her gaze on her paper. "I took it to get polished this morning."

"Oh." Ava frowned. "When should I pick it up?"

"It will be a while." She glanced up, giving a smile, though Ava caught how tight the edges of her mouth were. "Don't worry about it."

Ava nodded, wondering if that was true. She'd caught Harriet eyeing the lamp, among several other items around the office, before glancing back at her accounting ledger. If Ava remembered correctly, the lamp had belonged to a grandparent of Harriet's. Could she have sold a family heirloom?

The remainder of the day passed quickly, though quietly. It was what Ava dubbed a "ghost day." One in which Harriet only left her office for lunch, and that was only because Ava practically dragged her into the kitchen. These days gave Ava time to take care of things around the apartment, but the cavernous quiet also filled her with wonder for Harriet. She watched Harriet chew her lip as she worked, stubborn determination on her face. Each time Ava steeled herself to ask if Harriet wanted help, uncertainty reared its head, and she would back down. It was probably for the best. Offering assistance in such a personal matter wasn't a good way to remain professional. She was here to do a job, and that was it. Though, after the lamp business this morning, curiosity—that was what it still was, she was certain—intensified.

When she placed a sandwich tray next to Harriet that evening before leaving, she said, "Don't forget to take a break."

Harriet finished scribbling a note before leaning back in her chair. The curtains at the window were still open. Fading sunlight cast a strange glow over the room. She stretched, finding Ava's gaze. "You're leaving?"

"It's six o'clock."

Glancing wide-eyed at her clock, Harriet nodded. "So it is." She shook her head, yawning slightly. "Ava, I..." She seemed to search her face. Ava swallowed at Harriet's eyes lingering on her lips. "Thank you, for the sandwich."

"I'll see you in the morning."

Downstairs, Ava waved to Bert and remembered something. "Oh." She wandered over to the main elevator where he stood. His gray hair looked freshly cut under his doorman's hat, giving him a distinguished air. "Do you mind telling me where Miss Browning brought her lamp?" At his confused brow, she added, "She dropped it off this morning, and I want to make sure I pick it up on time." Harriet was probably too preoccupied to think about things like that if it was true.

"Apologies, Miss Clark, but I'm afraid I don't follow."

"Miss Browning, didn't she come down this morning? She had a Tiffany lamp with her. She went to get it polished."

"I'm afraid Miss Browning wasn't down here this morning." His dark eyes lit up. "I did see a warehouseman come down the back stairs with a beautiful Tiffany lamp."

Ava struggled to understand. Had somebody come to pick it up? That was something she could have done. Unless...

Bert leaned closer, his tone worried. "To be honest, Miss Browning hasn't left that apartment since early April."

"April?" Ava stepped back. "But she told me..." She pictured Harriet's lowered gaze as she had mentioned the lamp. The drop in her tone. Of course, Ava thought. *I was right.* She returned to Bert's comment. "Not since April?"

"Not that we've seen."

Ava nodded. "Thank you."

The next week, on the second Tuesday in June, Ava decided to test if what Bert said was true. She'd known Harriet was acting different. She was stressed, undoubtedly, and always working, but it seemed impossible that she'd been inside for over a month. Only oddballs and people who were ill stayed inside for that long. Harriet Browning wasn't either of those things. She wasn't who she once was, but that didn't make her a hermit.

On the subway, Ava had seen flyers for New York City's Fourth of July parade. Perfect, she thought. It was a fun excuse to be outside. Besides, Harriet was probably already involved. She recalled the summer between years at Briarcliff, when she'd stood on the Mars float beside Harriet and some of their school friends, joyfully waving to thousands of spectators as trumpets played and soldiers marched down the streets of Manhattan. Images from later that night danced out from forgotten corners of her mind when she reached Harriet's apartment and stepped out of the elevator.

A sharp crash broke Ava from her reverie. She hurried into the kitchen to find Harriet crouching over a broken plate. "Are you all right?"

Harriet was still in her robe. She looked tired as she placed the broken dish into a bucket Ava fetched. "You're late," was all she said.

"The train was late, not me," she replied, though her grin

was met with a withering glare. "Rough night?" she asked, helping scoop the final pieces into the bucket.

"I'm fine."

Ava dumped the shards into the trash, glancing back to find Harriet staring forlornly where the shattered plate had lain. "You know," she said, trying to sound chipper, "the Fourth of July parade is in a couple weeks. What do you say we head down to watch it that morning? That is to say, as long as you're not already booked. I'm sure you're helping to organize a dozen things that day."

Harriet only blinked, then slowly stood. She looked strangely small in the middle of her kitchen, clutching the collar of her robe. "What?"

"Aren't you a part of those committees? You know, with the other fancy women of New York?" She grinned, but it faltered as Harriet continued to stare.

"I resigned from the parade organization committee three years ago."

"Oh." Ava placed her hands on her hips. "Well, which float will they have you on this year?"

Harriet's jaw clenched. She moved past Ava briskly, starting to wash her hands at the sink. "I wasn't invited to be a part of it." She paused. "I imagine you already knew that since you handle my correspondence."

Her sharp tone made Ava's throat go dry. She hadn't seen anything about it but had figured such things were planned months in advance, before she was working here.

"I didn't mean to offend you. I only thought—"

"You thought you know my life, but you don't." She slammed the faucet off. Ava was too stunned to reply when Harriet stalked out of the kitchen. Over her shoulder, she called, "I'll be working. Please don't bother me until lunch," and disappeared down the hall.

Ava stared at the doorway, then the floor where the dish had been. The idea that Harriet was cracking under the pressure of things struck Ava as she found a rag mop and ran it over the kitchen floor. That had to be the reason for her behavior. Still, she didn't have to be so terse about things. Wasn't that why Ava was here, to be of help? Instead, Harriet had brushed her aside, not even giving her the chance to do so. Sighing, Ava leaned against the mop handle. Very well. If Harriet was going to act that way, two could play that game. Ava put away the mop, grabbed Harriet's latest to-do list, and got to work.

❖

It wasn't until Friday that Harriet worked up the nerve to greet Ava at the elevator when she arrived.

"Sorry I'm late," Ava said, a wary look cutting to Harriet as she unpinned her hat and hung up her jacket, revealing a canary yellow blouse over blue trousers. "Summer in the city, packed with tourists overloading the trains."

"It's no trouble." Harriet smiled and tried not to be offended by Ava's confused look. "Coffee?"

They went into the kitchen. Ava sat by the window, pushing herself as far back from the table as possible. Harriet fetched two mugs of coffee, then sat across from Ava. She quietly relished the way Ava's gaze flickered over her dress and sweater combination. It was the first fresh outfit she'd worn in four days. "I want to apologize," she finally said, cupping her already half-empty mug. "For the other day. I was terrible and shouldn't have lashed out at you."

Ava licked her lips, her gaze holding Harriet's. She raised a brow but didn't say anything.

"I, well, it's true what I said about my social life and its changes." She chuckled nervously, reaching up to fiddle with the end of her pearl necklace. "Since Father died and Mother left, the invitations have dwindled."

"Your correspondence seems ample enough."

"It's not what it was. Throw in my divorce…" She took a sip, wincing at the overload of sugar she'd added. "Well, people became busy when I called. Scar is the only one who will see me now."

Ava tapped the side of her mug before slowly turning it.

"What?" Harriet asked, unable to keep from smiling, knowing Ava had a question.

Her eyes stayed down when she asked, "Is it true you haven't left this apartment since April?"

The midmorning light seemed to intensify, making her squint. She shifted as her throat dried. A familiar, low panic struck in her gut. The frenzy reached her mind, and she moved to stand.

A cool hand, firm but gentle, held her wrist. She stared at Ava's hand keeping her from retreating. The image broke open an old box of memories. Her kitchen transformed to her dorm room at Briarcliff. It was littered with neatly taped boxes, the bed stripped, her life packed up for her journey to Lawrence's home following their soon-to-be wedding.

Ava's hand had held hers then, too, but the grasp had been angry, desperate. Harriet recalled her own searing sense of agony at the look in Ava's tear-filled eyes after Harriet had told her she was engaged.

"Harriet."

The sound of her name tore her from the past. She was home. Ava still held her wrist, though her hand retreated as if to match the timidness drawn over her face.

Settling back into the seat, Harriet sighed. She flattened

the hair behind her ear, though she knew it was already in place. "I went to the park once. Early April, I believe it was." *I only stayed for five minutes, but you don't need to know that.*

"How long has it felt like this?" Ava asked. "Like you can't go outside?"

Harriet fidgeted. Agitation climbed up her legs, and she fought the urge to squirm. She hadn't talked about this with anyone. She found, though, that it felt as if the words had been lingering, waiting in the depths of her chest for somebody to ask. They flowed freely from her lips. "After Father died, things stayed the same for a year or so. I made appearances at events. But once Mother left in '43, the invitations seemed to go with her. I continued to donate and host events." At Ava's curious look, she explained, "We didn't realize there wasn't any money to donate. I wouldn't have given what I had, had I known." She sighed. "The mills closing caught my attention, and I began to look over Father's books. Things didn't seem right, so I organized a meeting with his advisors. Now, here we are."

Across from her, Ava nodded, her gaze sympathetic.

"Now, I've been dealing with this mess," she said, gesturing to the hallway. "I've not time for anything else. You know how I can get when I'm working. Sometimes, I'd paint for days at a time."

"You're not painting, though." Ava sat back. "That kit of yours hasn't been touched in a long time by the look of the dust gathering atop it."

"How could I with all this?"

A small line between her brows, Ava said, "You've got to get out sometime."

"I don't see why. There's no one out there dying to see me. I'm a divorced heiress in financial straits. The press would have a field day if they got their hands on my picture."

"That's why you stay in? Since when did an embellished social page intimidate you?" At Harriet's silence, she added, "People still call on you. It seems to me you're choosing not to see them."

Harriet's eyes widened. Mouth open, she could only scoff, turning her head to stare out the window, anywhere but at Ava Clark.

"It's natural that people would worry about you if they haven't seen you in some time. It's also normal for the women of your world to gossip for the same reason. What's wrong with a stuffy tea with some of them to dispel any rumors?"

The low panic wriggled into a defensive stance. "They don't want to know I'm well. I know intimately how high society works. I've seen it happen time and again the last fifteen years. One misstep is all it takes, and you're a pariah. It's like you never existed," she added, her voice catching. She couldn't help picturing the Vanderbilts and their downfall. She and her mother had been among the very people looking down upon them from what they had thought was a stable perch. Only now did Harriet realize how tenuous her own stature in society had been and how hypocritical she was.

Ava crossed her arms. "But there hasn't been a misstep as far as they're concerned," she said, pointing to the skyscrapers outside. "Nobody knows about your money problems."

"Oh, they'll make assumptions. They'll see my donations dropping off, which they have. Each mill that closes makes the paper. Better to head them off at the pass," she said, grimacing at the phrase her mother had obtained from Buck.

They sipped their coffee. Harriet felt Ava studying her before she softly asked, "You sold the Tiffany lamp, didn't you?"

Harriet set her cup down harder than she intended, startled again by Ava's keen ability to know the truth. She nodded.

"Okay." Ava downed the rest of her coffee. "Well, I still think you should reconsider." Harriet frowned. "July Fourth. We could sit out front, near the doors. The parade marches right through here."

"I don't know."

Ava gave half a grin. "The Harriet Browning I knew wouldn't be afraid of ladies in tea hats gossiping into their telephones."

"The Harriet Browning you knew was a naive girl."

They were quiet a minute. Eventually, Ava stood. She motioned to take Harriet's mug, then held her hand in place. "Think about it?"

Harriet wasn't sure if it was Ava's fingers over hers or the faint playful spark in her eyes that nudged that opening of hope in her chest wider. Whatever it was, she smiled and dipped her chin. "I'll consider it."

"Good." Ava nodded to the hall. "I'll wash up. You go on. You've got work to do." Watching Ava, Harriet settled back into her seat. A sense of ease wrapped around her, and for a moment she imagined it was Ava's arms pulling her close, holding her tight. She shook her head. *Nonsense.* Ava was being kind. She couldn't confuse kindness with anything else. Regardless, Harriet was grateful for Ava, and for the first time in a long time, she was looking forward to a holiday.

CHAPTER FOURTEEN

Yoo-hoo, H!"

"I've got to tell Bert to telephone when she shows up like this," Harriet mumbled, adding a final dab of mascara to her lashes. She straightened to check her reflection, smoothing her blue and white striped dress. She flattened the Peter Pan collar and adjusted the large white bow sitting on her left hip. It accented a belt that gave her lithe figure the semblance of a waist. She was eyeing the row of lipsticks on her vanity when Scarlett fluttered into the bathroom.

"Darling, you look absolutely fabulous! Like an American treasure."

Turning, they exchanged air kisses before Harriet was turned and grabbed by the waist. Scarlett held her at arm's length. "Truly, dear, you look lovely."

"As do you," she said, taking in Scarlett's bold red romper. She wore matching heels and a white headband to keep back her hair. "What're you doing here, anyway? Shouldn't you be with Martha and Sally on the General Foods float?"

Scarlett checked her own makeup in the mirror. "I've got a few minutes. I had to come wish you a Happy Fourth. Lawrence says hello."

"Hello, Lawrence. Where's he today?"

"With some Hollywood tart upstate." She rolled her eyes.

"I told him after your divorce that he'd never find another woman like you."

Harriet snorted, scrunching her face as she continued to study the lipsticks. "For his sake, I hope not."

They laughed. "I also came to see if I could convince you to join me, but you seem to have your own plans." She gave Harriet a bump with her hip.

Harriet pretended to read the label on one of her lipsticks. "It's nothing. Just going out to watch you and everyone else float by."

When Scarlett was quiet, Harriet finally looked up to find her grinning. "This is Ava's doing, isn't it?"

"Oh, hush." Harriet felt heat fill her cheeks.

"I knew I liked her from the moment I met her."

Harriet had picked up one lipstick shade when Scarlett quickly handed her another. "This one." She winked. "It's an irresistible color."

"Thanks."

"The parade starts at ten. Is that when you'll go down?"

Harriet nodded. "As soon as Ava's here. She's been late the last week. Those trains never seem to run on time."

"From where does she commute?"

"Brooklyn."

"I'm impressed she's ever on time. The trains from there are a mess."

Dabbing her lips, Harriet laughed. "You know Brooklyn?"

Scarlett lifted her chin. "I pride myself on knowing all of this magnificent city." Then she checked her wristwatch. "Well, I must be off." They stood facing the mirror. Scarlett nudged her shoulder. "You look radiant."

"You'll be late, Scar."

"I expect to hear all about it. I'll wave to you when we pass by."

At five after ten, Ava practically flew out of the elevator. "I'm sorry I'm late. The entire city is here for the parade." A thin sheen of perspiration glistened on her forehead and at the back of her neck as she hung up her hat and handbag. Harriet gazed down Ava's fitted, white cotton shirt she wore over her usual blue trousers with a pair of low heels. She'd styled a victory roll on one side of her head, the rest of her hair glamorously pinned high for the warm day.

Harriet's mouth went dry as she stood in the hallway, and Ava closed the elevator. "You look…" Her words fumbled when Ava glanced over her shoulder on her way to the kitchen. "Patriotic."

Ava chuckled. "Likewise." Harriet followed. "I'll get some thermoses of iced tea ready. Bert has two chairs set up for us. The parade passes by here starting at ten twenty."

"Ten twenty." She checked her watch. A faint, tight sensation clenched low in her stomach, but she ignored it, focusing on the whirlwind that was Ava gathering items into a picnic basket.

Wringing her hands, Harriet glanced from Ava to the window. It was a clear day. Moving closer to look outside, she found the sidewalks below already packed with spectators. The feeling in her stomach spiked again, but she took a breath, trying to quell it.

"Ready?" Ava stood in the kitchen doorway, a wicker basket in her right hand, her left out to Harriet.

Crossing the room, Harriet took her hand. "Ready."

In the lobby, Bert greeted her enthusiastically. "Miss Browning, Happy Fourth! It's wonderful to see you." The other staff followed suit, flitting about her as if she was a rare bird.

"Our chairs, Bert?" Ava asked, gently guiding Harriet to the side doors that faced Central Park.

"Right this way, ladies."

Harriet smiled at Ava, grateful she kept them moving; she felt all eyes on her and her sudden emergence into the world. A few feet in front of the revolving doors, Harriet stopped.

Two plastic chairs with yellow cushions sat on the other side. Across the street, people stood four rows deep, men and women in their Sunday best with splashes of red, white, and blue dotting a sea of onlookers. Children sat on the curb, eating candy or skipping up and down the road, too fidgety to sit still and wait for the parade to begin. Others sat cross-legged, looking glum, utterly unimpressed with having to sit in the hot summer air. She used to be one of those people, out in the world, thriving.

"This way, Miss Browning." She was being ushered forward. Ava was already outside, setting the basket between the chairs. More thoughts raced through her mind, building into a high-pitched buzz. She used to be like everybody else, but she wasn't anymore. Was she? Could she be? Ava thought so, but was she really ready? Her heart seemed to quicken its pace.

"Bert, I—"

He nudged her into the space between glass partitions in the revolving door, and she was pushed awkwardly onward. For a brief moment within the revolving glass, everything was quiet. The hum of conversation from the lobby fell away, and she was encased in only the sound of her own breathing.

It was coming too quickly.

Bright sunlight dazzled her, but it was the noise that made her cry out. Hundreds of voices cheering at a volume she hadn't heard since...she couldn't recall. Everywhere, people. Somebody bumped into her, and she realized she was standing in the middle of the crowded sidewalk.

"Harriet."

She spun and found Ava, who took her hand and led her to their chairs positioned on a sidewalk square all to themselves.

Once they were seated, Ava asked, "Are you all right?"

She gave a smile but felt the tightening of her stomach expand to her chest. She placed a hand over her sternum to try to control her breathing.

A firecracker shot off on the street. Harriet yelped and nearly fell out of her chair. "I'm sorry," she said at Ava's concerned face. She was turned to face her, one hand on the back of her chair. "I'm fine."

"You don't look fine."

Still smiling, Harriet felt the panic rise in her throat. She could do this. She could be like all these people. She swallowed, trying to force the fear back down into her chest, but that only constricted her breathing more. "Truly, I…" But more people hurried by all around them. She thought she saw Mrs. McCarthy across the street. Was she laughing? Everything began to sound distorted, like when a record on her gramophone ended, the music coming to a scratching halt. "I'm all right," she said again. But she was hot, and her hand couldn't ease the rapid beating in her chest, and she grew lightheaded. "Maybe if I just—"

As soon as she stood, though, her vision narrowed, and she fell.

❖

"Imogene, I don't think people even have smelling salts anymore. This is 1948, not 1892."

"Well, it's what we always use when my mother faints at the start of the latest Gene Kelly flick."

Ava sighed and put the phone between her ear and shoulder as she continued to rifle through Harriet's kitchen.

She'd become so familiar with it, yet under the strain of the last fifteen minutes, she'd forgotten where everything was. "I'm not sure she really fainted. It seemed like something else."

"You said you were outside?"

"On the sidewalk right outside her building. I thought it would be nice for her to—" She cut herself off, not wanting to expand upon how she'd wanted to ease the strain of Harriet's life with a nice outing. "We were just waiting for the parade."

"Maybe the warm air got to her. It's brutal this time of year. She hasn't been outside in some time, right?"

Ava moved on to the icebox, the telephone cord wrapping around her legs as she sifted through slabs of meat wrapped in butcher paper. "Maybe I can press this to her forehead."

"You know," Imogene was saying, "Joe has a few friends who get like that, especially when they're in a crowd. Ever since they came home. He calls it a 'case of the nerves.'"

"She hasn't been to war, Imogene."

"No, but she's stressed, according to you. Combine that with not stepping outside in some time. Golly, I'd faint, too."

Ava grimaced, deciding to forgo the meat, opting for a rag she ran under cold water. "I'll call you later."

She hung up and hurried into the guest room. It was as far as she had been able to stumble with Harriet half-conscious on her arm after Bert had helped get them into the elevator. She'd drawn the curtains nearly closed, but a small opening let in a bold ray of midday light that streaked across the floor near the base of the bed. Harriet lay atop the covers, her back to the door.

Ava hesitated. She wanted to make sure Harriet was okay, but something about the way her legs were tucked close to her chest gave her pause. Harriet had been guarded since they'd started working together. Ava figured it was due to the stress of her family's finances weighing on her, but this morning had been different. Harriet had been eager, a glimmer of her former, effervescent self when Ava had arrived. Then, outside…Ava had never seen her as frantic as she'd been before she'd collapsed.

She stepped quietly forward, letting her gaze linger on the steady rise and fall of Harriet's shoulders. As she carefully laid the cold compress on her forehead, Harriet shifted.

"That feels nice." She moved to hold the rag as she turned onto her back. Her eyes were still closed. Thin streaks of mascara sat at the edges beneath them.

Ava swallowed the lump in her throat at the sight of Harriet's pulse point. "I wanted to make sure you were all right."

"Oh, it's mostly my pride that was wounded today. The little I had left, anyway."

"If it makes you feel better, only the front military trumpets had marched by when you went down."

"Excellent." Harriet took a long, deep breath.

"What happened out there?"

After what felt like minutes, Harriet's eyes fluttered open. She seemed to study the ceiling.

"Was it the crowd?" Ava stepped closer. "I probably should have considered that more. You haven't been outside, well, not really outside, in some time, and here I am throwing you into a throng of people. And on the Fourth of July, during a parade! I thought it would be fun. A break for you from all of your work. I didn't even think—"

"Ava."

She pursed her lips. "Sorry."

"It wasn't the crowds." She took another long breath. Ava sat near her legs, careful to keep a respectable distance. She waited as Harriet adjusted the compress. "When I was in the lobby, looking outside, all I could think about was how I've never sat on the side to watch the parade go by."

"Not even as a kid?"

"Not once. My father and mother had me in their car behind the Carnegies, most years. As a teenager, my friends and I would stand on the Hershey or Ford floats. I was always involved in some way. Even last year, I sat on the Delloite float, given out of sympathy more than anything." Her voice wavered. "I've never been as sidelined as I am now."

Ava bit her lip. "But, Harriet—"

"I know. I've sequestered myself away. I quit the committees."

"I'm sure it's been difficult." Ava frowned, trying to figure out where Harriet was going. Something didn't quite make sense. "Were you afraid you'd see somebody? Somebody you knew?"

Harriet slammed her eyes shut, tugging the compress down over them. "Maybe I was. God, I'm such a coward."

"You're no such thing." Ava reached out, gently taking the compress so Harriet had to look at her. "Do you hear me? You're just…going through a lot right now." Harriet searched her gaze. Ava felt hot beneath it but focused on the pain in Harriet's eyes to keep her grounded. "What?" she asked softly. "What is it?"

Harriet shifted to sit up. Ava's stomach squirmed, wondering what made her look so vulnerable. With her back against the headboard, Harriet resembled her old prim self, though the sadness in her gaze made Ava's chest ache.

"My father's money was tied up in a bank that didn't survive the Crash. He recovered most of the money but invested it poorly. Eventually, he decided to put this apartment up as collateral. Like his other deals, it fell through."

Ava looked from Harriet's bleary gaze to the doorway and back again. "You mean…"

Harriet nodded. "I have until the end of September to come up with the mortgage's equivalent, which I fear may be impossible. I've only the money my father left me, which over the last ten years has gone to charities and events. I never wanted money from Lawrence after our divorce. And the mills…well, you know about that." She gave a sad shrug. "Then, I suppose, the bank will take my home." Her voice broke on home, and she cried out, covering her face.

"Oh, Harriet." Ava moved forward, taking her hands. Harriet cried, her head hanging low. Ava pulled her into a hug. It made sense now. The hours in the office, the tense meetings, selling her possessions. For some time, Harriet Browning had been losing her footing in the world she'd known. Now, she was losing her home, too.

They were still hugging when Harriet shifted to face the window again. Her left hand slid down Ava's right arm, pulling her to follow. The gesture sent a flare of white-hot memory down Ava's spine. Her body knew what to do, and she fell behind Harriet on the bed. She pressed herself against Harriet's back, her left arm wrapped around her, holding her as she continued to cry.

"It'll be all right," she whispered, afraid at how fragile the bold, carefree Harriet Browning seemed in her arms. Ava wanted to help. She wanted to make her feel better, but Harriet was in her arms again, and that stalled her mind, stunting her thoughts. She closed her eyes to quiet the continuous, cautioning whistle in her ears and focused on holding Harriet, something she never thought she'd do again.

CHAPTER FIFTEEN

Harriet inhaled deeply upon waking. She didn't recall falling asleep. Blinking, confusion overtook her when she spotted the drab gray curtains of the guest room. The feeling deepened as soft orange light crept in where they were parted. How long had she been asleep?

A lovely, faint scent hit her: rose water, Ava's perfume. The warm thoughts it gave her were replaced by a surge of longing when she realized Ava's arm was around her waist. That surge threatened to overpower her, to make her grab Ava's hand and kiss her knuckles.

The thought nearly made her bolt upright. Quickly, Harriet slid out from under Ava. She bent to gather her shoes. Ava yawned on the bed. Harriet stepped back to the window, adding distance to squash the sudden rapid beating in her chest. "I'm afraid we fell asleep."

For a moment, Ava seemed content as she stretched, still on her back amid the pillows.

Harriet said, "It's morning."

At this, Ava's eyes shot open. She sat up, looking from Harriet to the bed. "Oh, my…Harriet, I'm sorry. I wanted to make sure you weren't alone since you were out of sorts. I didn't mean to drift off." She ran a hand through her hair, a startled look in her brown eyes. "That was completely unprofessional of me."

Ava's frantic movements as she began to smooth the blankets and rearrange the pillows made Harriet smile. Waking up in her arms had been unexpected, yes, but not unpleasant.

"Ava, it's all right. I appreciate your concern." She picked up a small throw pillow that had fallen and set it with the others. Ava ran a hand down her shirt, avoiding Harriet's gaze. "Well, since you're already here, care for breakfast?"

"I should run home. I need to shower and…" She trailed off, looking down. "I ought to change."

"There are plenty of washrooms here. And I'm sure there's a fresh shirt in my closet you can borrow." She smiled, telling herself not to stare at the adorable cowlick that had developed in Ava's hair as she'd slept. At Ava's contemplative look, Harriet ushered her into the hall. "Go on. Use my bathroom. I'll start breakfast."

Harriet had two pieces of toast in the oven when Ava came in. "What can I do to help?" she asked.

"Nothing at all. Here's a cup of coffee. Take a—" Harriet's words left her at the sight of Ava in a silk button-down. It was one she'd bought in London three summers ago, her last trip abroad. It was emerald green. On Harriet, it fit perfectly. Though perfect might have been the way it clung to Ava's bust. The top button was open due to the snug fit. Harriet snapped her eyes to Ava's amused gaze.

"Thanks," Ava said, taking her mug and sitting. Her hair was wet from the shower, brushed back from her face.

Harriet busied herself with the eggs she placed on the toast. Gathering butter and peach jam, she carried everything to the table.

"I thought that was my job." Ava sipped her coffee, a smile peeking out from behind her mug.

"It's the least I can do after yesterday." Harriet sat across from her. "I feel so foolish."

"You've put a lot of pressure on yourself." Ava licked her lips, and a hint of something else laced her voice. "I added to it by pushing you to do something before you were ready."

For a moment, their gazes met, and Harriet wondered if they were both picturing that day in her dorm room. *Is that how Ava felt about Briarcliff?*

"You had good intentions. It's me." She buttered her toast slowly. "It's always been me who wasn't ready."

Ava seemed to weigh her words. "Is that why you married Lawrence?"

The toast caught in her throat as she swallowed. Here was the question she'd been waiting fifteen years for. Despite all the preparation she had done in the hope of one day, maybe, being given the chance to explain herself, she felt adrift. She should have expected the unexpected when it came to Ava Clark, like asking the question over toast at breakfast.

"Ava…you have to understand. The pressure you speak of…back then, it was unbearable. I couldn't…" She faltered, setting the knife down. "I couldn't see another way."

Ava's nostrils flared, a flash of something lighting her eyes.

"My entire well-being depended on the men in my world. My father's money and name gave me everything until I was eighteen. It had been ingrained in me since birth that in order to continue on as I had, I had to marry. It was what I was supposed to do."

Ava took a bite, chewing slowly and holding Harriet's gaze. Harriet could practically see the dozens of questions floating through the morning light between them. Eventually, Ava asked, "Why did you divorce?"

Because I've always been in love with you. Harriet took

a sip of juice to force the words back down. She couldn't say that. It wouldn't be fair. Even though Ava was here, they weren't what they were. Harriet had hurt her. The chances that Ava could ever feel anything for her again were impossible. She wouldn't care that Harriet had thought about her every day since graduation. It was Ava she remembered. Ava whom she thought about at night. It had always been her since Harriet made the worst mistake of her life in giving her up.

"We couldn't give each other what we needed," she finally said, giving a small shrug.

Ava watched her a moment more. As they sat there, Harriet tried to hold her gaze, hoping Ava would see how sorry she was, how she wished she could take it all back. Marrying Lawrence had been an act of cowardice. Nothing had rivaled the two years spent with Ava at Briarcliff. Nothing ever would. Still, Harriet wouldn't risk this new bond, as tenuous and far from her true desires as it was; she had to carry on if she wanted Ava in her life.

To push the conversation along, she said lightly, "Divorce seems to run in my family. You're lucky. Your parents always seemed idyllic. Married since they were young, living and working together on their land."

Ava's posture changed. Her shoulders fell, and she seemed interested in gathering all of the crumbs on her plate. She kept her gaze lowered as she finished her coffee.

"Ava?"

Her eyes shone when she cut her gaze to the window.

"Ava, what is it?"

"I haven't spoken to my parents in nearly three years."

Harriet would've dropped her coffee had she been holding it. Ava Clark adored her family. It had been one of the things that had drawn Harriet to her, the way the Clarks seemed to get along and truly share an affection for one another. Harriet recalled sitting on the bed, reading a fashion magazine in her dorm room while Ava wrote her monthly letter home. She scoured her mind as to why this might have changed.

"I went home eight years ago for William's funeral. When I came back to New York, everything seemed dim. I threw myself into work. Christmas of '44 was the last time I went back. Right after—" She cleared her throat. "Right after we received word about James."

Harriet didn't have siblings. She'd never had what she'd learned later in life was a "typical family." Letters home, family dinners, joshing around with a brother; it had all been foreign to her prior to meeting Ava. The few times she'd seen her with James, it was clear the siblings were close. She could only imagine the pain at having lost all that, could picture Ava alone with her parents. No wonder she wanted to avoid it.

"Since then, I haven't...I can't bring myself to go back. Besides, I'm not a war hero. I was a filing clerk while those boys were giving their lives overseas. Before that, I'd only had odd jobs here and there." She shook her head. "I couldn't even pay my rent before coming here. That's not the life I want my parents to know. They've dealt with enough."

Harriet was an expert in a thousand social settings. She knew how to handle a wealthy old crone who'd had too much champagne and was babbling her husband's misdeeds to greedy ears. She knew how to discreetly dismiss a handsy banker's advances in a crowded room. She'd even managed to save her own mother's reputation when her gown had been stepped on at a fundraiser and was nearly torn off her backside. The number of ways she knew to gracefully salvage circumstances was endless.

The right words to say to Ava Clark, sitting across from her in her kitchen, looking utterly crestfallen? All Harriet could think to say was, "I'm so sorry."

After taking a shuddering breath and putting on a smile, Ava said, "Imogene says I'm being silly. That my parents, who keep writing despite my not replying the last year, would welcome me home with open arms."

"She's probably right." Harriet smiled. "Imogene was that spunky, petite blond always lurking around the boys' college?"

Ava barked a laugh. "That's her." Her mood seemed to lift, and she pushed back her plate. "Enough sob stories. You, Miss Browning, have a dilemma with the mess your father left."

Harriet used her napkin to flick at Ava for her use of Miss Browning but found the new teasing tone a welcome one. She sighed, tapping the table next to her mug. "I have another meeting in a week and a half."

"Would you care for another set of eyes on those numbers?"

Harriet felt a blush creep up her neck at the offer she'd been too stubborn to ask for since her last meeting with Mr. Gray and Mr. Curtis. "You wouldn't mind?"

Ava's eyes seemed lighter above her smile. "I'd be happy to. All part of the job, right?"

Something in her voice made Harriet tilt her head. She considered the light playing in Ava's gaze, the way her nose crinkled a little when she smiled. *We're colleagues*, she reminded herself, but she was unable to keep her gaze from finding the curve of Ava's breast in that blouse.

"Right," she managed to reply. "All part of the job."

CHAPTER SIXTEEN

Over the next week, Ava spent the hours from three to six p.m. in Harriet's office. On Monday, she used the large leather sofa to take a look at the documents Harriet provided. She spent so much time walking back and forth to the desk that by Wednesday, she'd dragged in a dining room chair to sit opposite Harriet.

"Much easier this way, don't you think?" Harriet asked, offering Ava another glass of iced tea.

Ava agreed and had to admit she rather liked spending the latter half of her day near Harriet. Since the aftermath of the Fourth, a new sense of comfort had grown between them. Though, if she really thought about it, Ava knew it was the old, nearly forgotten ease with which they'd always interacted. It's like college, she found herself thinking on Thursday after they'd gone over the ledger from Harriet's father's mills, bouncing ideas off one another like lifelong business partners.

These thoughts towered over her like the skyscrapers in the outside world, though, marring her vision. As appealing as it was to lose herself in the simple rhythm of being around Harriet, it also jabbed dully at the scars across her heart. This was the woman who had torn her apart, left her a floundering mess on the day that should have been the start of their lives together. How, then, could Ava be enjoying Harriet's company once more?

She did her best to focus on the daily tasks instead of getting emotional. Despite her sharp eye for spotting discrepancies in calculations, Ava had to admit that Harriet's financial situation was, in fact, very grim.

"I'm sorry," she said that evening, sitting back from the pile of documents and scratch paper littered with figures she'd helped Harriet make sense of. "There really isn't any way around this."

Across from her, Harriet had her elbows on the desk, her head in both hands. She gave a long sigh. "I really thought we'd find something."

A flutter near her ribs at "we" made Ava straighten in her seat. "So did I. But it seems Mr. Gray and Mr. Curtis have their numbers correct." She drummed the desk as Harriet frowned, casting a sad look around the room. When she stood, heading for the telephone box in the corner, Ava was still combing her mind for something to help, but the only end to this she saw was the bank taking the apartment. She recalled old conversations with Harriet mentioning other homes abroad, but that idea gave Ava a startling and strange sensation of gloom. Staring at the mill ledgers, she frowned at the little money those seemed to bring in. Only seven of the original twenty-three were still in operation. Two more closed this month, and one was scheduled to shut down by August.

Even if Harriet had to give up the apartment, there had to be some way to come out of this without a complete loss. Ava glanced around at the fine marble busts and dozens of literary collections.

"What about an auction?" She said it more to herself, then remembered Harriet was across the room. Turning, she found her in mid-conversation on the phone.

"Yes, tomorrow night. Seven thirty. Bring whatever you like...No, we don't need that many bottles, Scar...I'll have a roast with vegetables...Just four...Great. See you then."

"Scarlett's coming by?"

Harriet still had her hand on the receiver, an odd smile on her face. "She's coming to dinner tomorrow. What's Imogene's number?"

Ava gave it to her, then asked, "She's coming, too?"

"Of course. She's lovely, and three is such an odd number for dinner, don't you think?"

Ava looked from the messy desk to Harriet, who vigorously dialed. "This is tomorrow?"

"Yes. I'm feeling like a dinner party. We need a bit of fun after all of this."

Ava opened her mouth to reply, but could only watch Harriet speak animatedly to what must have been a very confused Imogene. Slowly, she recognized Harriet's behavior. It was like the time she'd been overwhelmed studying for her impressionist art final, and she'd grabbed Ava out of bed, and they'd sprinted out to the lake for a midnight swim, anything to keep her mind from the daunting task awaiting her.

The auction idea could wait. Not long, but Ava decided one night of fun was something Harriet Browning did, in fact, desperately need. She crossed her arms, realizing this was the same feeling that had prompted the idea for the Fourth. Even before then, during the dinner where Imogene had asked after Harriet's affairs, she'd felt it. Ava wanted to protect Harriet. She'd wanted to keep her safe, make her smile. Hugging her own waist, Ava leaned back, running her gaze across the row of cabinets. She thought it would be fleeting, a momentary reaction to what Harriet was going through. But it lingered, curling around that sealed box in her mind, tugging it forward once again.

"It's just dinner," she said to herself, moving to stand while Harriet chatted away. Dinner with friends—employers—was perfectly acceptable.

Wasn't it?

❖

"You mean your children are always at home? *With* you?" Scarlett sat, mouth agape, in her seat at the long dining room table. In apparent shock, one hand on her chest—which had been wrapped in a mink shawl upon arrival that had later revealed a low-cut blue dress—she stared across the table at Imogene.

"Yes," Imogene replied, covering her mouth after a bite of Brussels sprout. "They're with their father most of the day while I'm at my stenographer job. But only until they go back to primary school in the fall."

Ava couldn't hide her grin as she sat at one end of the table, nearest the kitchen. Scarlett was looking at Imogene like she had three heads after learning all about her life. At the far end, Ava caught Harriet watching her and smiling at the amusing exchange.

"My, how positively modern." Scarlett took a sip from her red wine. "I can't even imagine. My husband, Paul Sachs, wouldn't be caught within five miles of his children. They're his from a previous marriage, mind you. I simply adore them; little Elizabeth and…" She paused.

"Marjorie?" Harriet finished for her.

"Precisely. But I'm afraid they're in Switzerland for school. And currently summering in France with their other mother."

"That sounds positively glamorous," Imogene replied.

She appeared equally rapt, if not also a bit frightened by Scarlett and her exuberant dinner conversation. Ava had been content to sit back and listen as Imogene asked questions about Scarlett's upbringing in Mississippi and leaving home to marry a wealthy northerner when she was seventeen.

Ava hardly noticed when the conversation turned to automobiles, and Scarlett asked her a question. "I'm sorry?"

"Do your parents have a car on their farm?"

"Oh, um, yes. A '35 Buick. They only use it to go into town."

Scarlett beamed. "How pastoral."

Ava laughed, saying, "It's not like the trains in New York, that's for sure."

"Though they've been awful about timeliness since summer began," Imogene interjected. "I've been nearly late to work five times. And I only have two stops on my ride."

Ava nodded, adding dryly, "It's a miracle Harriet hasn't docked my pay for all of my late arrivals."

Harriet smiled as Scarlett turned to Ava. She wore a mischievous grin before saying, "Harriet would never. Besides, I hear you're too valuable to ever consider letting go."

The comment surprised her. Harriet was red and cut intensely into the last piece of lamb on her plate. Glancing at Imogene, Ava caught her knowing gaze over the rim of her glass.

"You could stay here."

All of them froze. Ava wasn't sure she'd heard right as she watched Harriet who, after seeming to steel herself, met her gaze. "As you've all been saying, the trains aren't ideal. Wouldn't it make things easier if you were already here? Just until September when"—she glanced at Scarlett—"when you'll be free to move on."

Ava was sure she could hear a pin drop. Imogene swallowed more wine, shooting her wide-eyed looks. Meanwhile, Scarlett looked like the cat who'd caught the canary.

"What a generous offer," Scarlett said, breaking the silence. "H, dear, you are too kind."

"That is very kind," Ava managed to say, focusing on the glazed meat and not on the hopeful look in Harriet's eyes. She hardly heard the remainder of the dinner conversation and was grateful there was no dessert. Her mind buzzed like the electric streetlamps outside. Harriet was only being nice, she told herself. The commute had become rather tiresome, and she was often late. It would be convenient to wake up and simply walk into the next room to begin her workday. A glance at Harriet, though, sent a spike of something through her chest: a mix of fear and something else…hope?

"What're you going to do?" Imogene whispered after dinner as Ava helped with her hat.

She shrugged. "It would make things easier."

"Ava."

"I know. Trust me, I know," she said emphatically, keeping her voice low. Scarlett was talking to Harriet, who cleared the dishes into the kitchen. "It's been good, though. We've been working well together."

Imogene looked up at her, her big blue eyes worried. "I just don't want to see you hurt again."

Ava smiled. "You and me both. But you heard her. It's only for a couple months. Besides, I couldn't leave Mr. Wakowski without his lemon bars forever."

Imogene gave her an emphatic hug, whispering, "Be careful," before she left, Scarlett right behind her.

"It was lovely seeing you again, Ava. Your friend is an absolute delight. I'm going to invite her round for tea."

"Splendid." Ava waved, then went to help Harriet in the

kitchen. Motioning her to step aside, Ava took over washing plates, handing each to Harriet to dry. "Did you have a nice night?"

Harriet's smile was wide. "I really did."

"Good." Ava focused on the suds as she scrubbed raspberry glaze from a dish.

"I know it was frivolous of me," Harriet said after a minute. "I already owe the butcher and grocer, but I couldn't stand the utter doldrums my life has become. I needed something different, but still, you know, safe." She glanced at the windows. "Something—"

"Comfortable?" Ava passed her the last dish.

Harriet held her gaze. "Yes, exactly." She blinked, looking as if she'd lost herself momentarily. "Not that having you here makes things bleak. Quite the opposite, actually."

Ava focused on rinsing the wineglasses. They worked in companionable silence for a time. Ava turned Harriet's proposal to move in over in her mind. It was for convenience purposes, surely. Harriet didn't like her secretary running late each morning. That was the bottom line, Ava thought, watching the bubbles swirl around inside the sink. There was nothing more to it.

Harriet must have sensed her thoughts, saying, "I apologize for my forwardness at dinner." Ava glanced sideways. "Asking you if you'd move in was a personal question." She faltered, quickly adding, "And for an entirely professional purpose, of course. I only intended to offer a suitable alternative. I realize I put you on the spot, though, in front of Scar and Imogene."

"You did." Ava turned, finding a mildly surprised look on Harriet's face. Passing her the last glass, she dried her hands. "But it's all right. I know you meant well." She turned to face Harriet, who dried the last of the glasses. "Do you think..." She licked her lips, watching those lithe fingers adjust the base of each glass, lining them up on the counter. "I mean...you wouldn't mind?"

"Of course not. I'd be...I mean, I wouldn't want you to be bothered anymore with running to and fro if you can help it." She gestured to the kitchen. "And here is a perfectly oversize apartment with ample room to spare. Besides, it would only be temporary."

Ava recalled their initial phone conversation. Temporary. Right. All of this was limited time. It seemed strange, like their days together thus far had been simultaneously compressed and expanded. It was old and new.

And it was time she'd enjoyed.

Reaching out, she adjusted the collar of Harriet's dress, not entirely certain what compelled her to do so.

Harriet's voice seemed lower when she asked, "What do you say?"

Ava smiled, admiring the light in Harriet's eyes. It had been a long time since she'd really looked into them, and she found a new depth to the shades of blue. "I'll think about it," she finally said, moving into the hallway to fetch her things.

Harriet followed. At the elevator, she tucked a stray hair behind her ear. Was she nervous? "I'll be happy to write your Mr. Wakowski, too, to explain the situation."

"Thanks." They stood waiting, Ava with one hand on the elevator gate. A tension enveloped them. It felt strangely like the end of a first date, and Ava was hit with a wave of nerves. "Well, have a good weekend."

"You too. See you Monday."

Ava stepped in, closing the gate behind her. As the elevator descended, she fell back against the wall. It struck her sharp and sudden like a bell, startling her with its clarity: over the next two days, she was going to miss Harriet Browning.

Chapter Seventeen

The last Monday in July, Harriet opened the elevator to find Ava with an old but very full suitcase at her side. A thrilling elation sprang from Harriet's feet to her head, and she tried to contain it in a smile. "Welcome."

"Last week was the nail in the coffin. Truly, who brings livestock onto the train? The entire ride was shut down for an hour while the conductor sorted things out. Not to mention the cleanup after." Ava carried her bag into the guest room, then met Harriet in the kitchen.

"I did see that in the paper. Scar was delighted. I think she's trying to pitch it as a movie idea to Lawrence's new starlet paramour." Harriet handed her coffee.

She snorted. "I'd see that one. I hope it stars Cary Grant." She seemed to hesitate before adding, "I'll be sure not to get in your hair while I'm here. And it would probably be wise to write that letter to Mr. Wakowski. I left him a new batch of lemon bars, but he still seemed concerned by my suitcase."

Harriet nodded but was lingering on Ava's words. Specifically, her "not wanting to get in Harriet's hair." She found herself wanting quite the opposite, to have Ava's hands on her. She took a breath, chasing the image away only for it to be replaced by the memory of her own fingers tugging through Ava's locks. Harriet shook her head, refocusing. Today, Ava's hair was pinned elegantly behind her ears, the rest of it cascading gently just past her shoulders. She recalled a time when she'd taken hold of those locks and—

"Harriet?"

"Hmm?" She blinked and felt the heat that had nestled in her abdomen rush to her face.

"Do I have something in my hair?" She picked at her ends, frowning.

"Oh, no. Sorry." She moved to the counter. "I believe I need more coffee. Still waking up."

Fortunately, after her mental lapse, Harriet fell back into her easy working rhythm with Ava. Around midday, Ava proposed an auction of the Browning estate items, as those were the majority of the possessions in the apartment. Ava had run the rough hypothetical numbers after Harriet had provided what she thought the major pieces could be worth. It likely would just barely equate to the mortgage, providing a little extra that would give Harriet a comfortable foundation to begin again, wherever that might be.

That was an aspect of all this Harriet dreaded to ponder: where she'd end up when all was said and done.

"You don't want to join your mother on the ranch?" Ava asked, a teasing tone floating across the office later that day. She stood near the corner fireplace, notepad in hand as she listed the items on the mantel.

"A visit I could do. But a long-term stay with Velma, Buck, and the cows?" She straightened a pile of paperwork on the desk. "I don't think anyone would fare well."

Ava chuckled. "Is it because his name is Buck?"

"No. Though, truly, what were his mother and father thinking?" Harriet shook her head. "Admittedly, he does seem to make my mother happy. He must, for I see no other reason why she'd move her entire life to the desert, forgoing the only home she'd known for decades."

"You've met him, haven't you?" Ava asked, twirling her pencil.

"About a year after my father's funeral. Mother had just moved down there. He's kind, looks a bit like Spencer Tracy, or Spencer Tracy's rustic cousin. Either way, he was a complete fish out of water on the visit. Still, Mother showed him off to all her friends, and they absolutely adored him. Then they rode off into the Nevada sunset."

Ava watched her, half a smile on her face. "Velma and the cowboy. Now that's a motion picture idea."

Harriet laughed. "All that to say, he's perfectly respectable, but I'd rather not book an extended stay on the ranch if I can help it."

Ava turned, one hand on her hip as she asked, "Where are your other properties again?"

"Mother was left the villa in France." She glanced down. "I could go there."

"It's far."

Harriet looked up, wondering at the look in Ava's eyes. "It is. There's also the home in San Francisco."

She smiled. "That sounds promising."

"It's nearer some of the mills still in operation, which would be good. I could oversee things a bit more. Besides," she added, "it's not like I have a lot of options."

"I suppose not." She placed a hand in her trouser pocket. The motion drew Harriet's gaze.

Clearing her throat, she said, "I've been meaning to ask, why do you still wear those?" She gestured to Ava's black pants that fell over fashionable if outdated boots. "The war's over. Material is available again for skirts and dresses."

Ava quirked a brow. "You don't like them?"

Her gaze lingered a moment on the way the material accentuated the curve of Ava's hips. "I didn't say that."

"Your tone implied it."

Harriet met her gaze, taken aback. She crossed her arms, giving a small smile. "I forget how long it's been. You could read my tones better, once upon a time."

Ava pursed her lips, once again studying her notepad, though the skin around her eyes crinkled, and she couldn't seem to stifle a smile. "Well, I can tell your tastes haven't changed." She moved closer, placing the notepad in her left hand as she stood next to Harriet's chair. Reaching out, she plucked the elbow of Harriet's dress sleeve. She ran her fingers up her arm, finding her collar, which she traced delicately. "You always did love a bold floral pattern."

The room seemed to shrink, pressing the air—and them—closer. Harriet reminded herself to breathe. Ava was merely recalling a fact. It didn't mean anything. But those beautiful eyes were holding hers, and a light tug of arousal kindled in her abdomen. She reached up, using every ounce of her strength, and moved Ava's hand away.

Dissatisfaction washed over her, but she couldn't move. She wanted to pull Ava down to her, kiss her, but she couldn't. Anything she saw in Ava's gaze, including what couldn't possibly be disappointment, was impossible.

"The pants suit you," she said hoarsely, scooting her chair closer to the desk.

Retreating to the other side of the office, Ava muttered, "Thanks," and returned to her work.

Soon after, Harriet excused herself and shut the door to her powder room. At the sink, she splashed her face.

How could she be so foolish? She'd been so blinded by wanting Ava in her life that she didn't see the consequences of its fruition. Ava being here all the time made it more difficult for Harriet to keep the feelings she had for her locked away. Those feelings had been dragged, biting and kicking, into a box she'd told herself to keep locked ever since her wedding day. She'd never thrown out the key, though, and it had become entirely too tempting lately to open it once again.

She'd been certain Ava couldn't possibly have a place like that in her mind. Harriet had thought she'd seen a glimpse of it just now, but no. It was only her own desperate longing reflected back at her.

Even if it was real, even if Ava could feel the same way, it was impossible now. Ava knew the truth of Harriet's situation. Even if they could pull things together for an auction, even if it was half a success, where did that leave them? Harriet would still be without a home. She'd be nobody, nothing without the power her name once held. That was the woman Ava knew, that was who Ava had loved once upon a time; Harriet Browning— socialite, heiress, American aristocrat. Harriet shuddered at the fear slinking through her mind; could anyone, especially Ava Clark, want whoever Harriet was to become once all was said and done?

She laughed, gripping the sink, at her keen ability to torture herself. "It's only temporary," she told her reflection, standing to adjust her bun. She was Harriet Browning. She'd handled a lot of things over the last fifteen years. Certainly, she could handle this.

Chapter Eighteen

The tension that had encased them in the study followed Ava to bed the first night, resulting in a fitful time trying to sleep. She feared what the following day might bring, especially since Harriet had retreated to her room and wasn't seen again till morning. But somehow, things were perfectly normal the next day. Ava even fell right asleep after a dinner of pheasant and charred cauliflower accompanied by a shared bottle of chardonnay. Perhaps it was partially thanks to the wine, but it was so easy to feel comfortable in the bed they'd once shared during those clandestine summer nights in 1932.

Unfortunately, that realization kept her up the third night. *It shouldn't be this easy.* She'd worked very hard for a long time to get over Harriet. She'd fought like hell to move on, forcing herself day after day not to think about the woman she'd fallen in love with at Briarcliff.

In the darkness, Ava rolled onto her back in bed, huffing at the ceiling. The last fifteen years of her life rolled by as if on a film reel. She saw the year after graduation and willed herself to move forward, her heart newly stitched together thanks to the support of her brothers and Imogene. She pictured a time with William, drinking beer on a muggy summer's night. They'd sat on the bumper of their parents' car, and he'd told her to forget Harriet. Though he'd never understood her affinity for women, he hadn't pushed her to go out with any of his friends. She was always grateful for that. "There are other fish in the sea," he had told her, "and what better sea than New York City?"

Later, James had been her wingman when Imogene was busy planning her wedding to Joe. They'd visited underground bars together, well after midnight, and she'd tried to lose herself in another woman's touch.

She remembered their last night together at his going-away party in a crowded apartment in Queens. They'd both been so eager, so full of life, thrilled at the other's prospects. She was about to move into her new apartment after working as a secretary for nine months; he was about to ship out to England.

The reel bubbled over, then flickered with the jarring image of William's coffin followed by the letter about James. She closed her eyes, tossing an arm over her face. Nothing had gone how she'd thought it would. She'd imagined a great life for herself, for her brothers. She'd imagined a future where they reunited with their parents around the kitchen table each Christmas, telling grand adventures from their lives. She'd pictured William married, James with at least four kids of his own, and her...well, she'd always imagined herself too busy for real love but content to visit home each year, money in her pocket and stories to tell.

The harsh reality was nothing like that. Her brothers weren't here. Until recently, she had barely been making ends meet, and as far as her heart went...well, it had been through a lot. She hadn't expected the last couple of months. Her employment hadn't even gone the way she'd planned. She'd confessed as much to Imogene on the phone when she'd told her she'd decided to move in. Her original intentions to show

Harriet what she'd been missing had crumbled like the facade Harriet Browning had put on for the world. It faltered before her, and Ava could see how much she'd had to deal with over the last decade, giving Ava an unexpected perspective. Harriet was not the bubbly, carefree debutante of long ago. She was simply a woman trying to do what she could to get by, not unlike Ava.

Closing her eyes, she pictured Harriet in her office chair. She once again felt the fine silk of Harriet's collar between her fingers. With that gesture, she'd unintentionally opened a door. Ava rolled onto her side. Or had she meant to open it? And if she did, what did that mean?

Years ago, Ava had imagined a future with Harriet. After graduating, they'd run away together. Travel the world. After all, a woman with Harriet's means could do whatever she wanted. Perhaps, after all, it had only been schoolgirl fantasies Ava had yearned for. Perhaps it hadn't really been possible. Now…what would they do? Ava had been struggling to earn a living and Harriet was, well, Harriet.

Ava flashed back to the summer she'd stayed here, the summer she'd been a part of Harriet's world, living among her family and friends. Another fantasy, a time that had come and gone that was, ultimately, never the life Ava could have lived forever. Even if they were on more even ground these days, ultimately, they were two women from very different worlds.

She decided to spend the next day avoiding her confusing thoughts by focusing on her inventory list. They'd agreed to compile all the art and literature from the office, gallery, and other guest rooms. These they'd have appraised, then sell at an auction come September.

When Harriet asked if she wanted to break for lunch at one, Ava declined. "I'd like to finish this lot." She pointed to the pile of encyclopedias.

Harriet nodded, but confusion lined her smile. "Of course. I'll save a tray for you."

She focused on her food at dinner, feigning exhaustion when she went to her room at nine, closing the door and collapsing in a heap of confusion. "Come on, Ava," she mumbled into the comforter. "Pull yourself together."

After a night of fitful sleep, she trudged to the kitchen the next morning. Pouring coffee, she jumped at Harriet's voice behind her.

"There you are. Do you mind?" She wore a powder-blue day dress and was reaching behind her toward the base of her neck. "The clasp is playing hard to get." She turned so Ava could close it. Ava studied the fair skin of Harriet's neck below her bun, finding she wanted to trace the light dotting of freckles with her lips.

"There you go."

"Thank you." She turned, and Ava noticed the dress matched her eyes. "Did you sleep all right?"

Ava shoved her previous thought away and shrugged. "You?"

"Pleasantly enough." She seemed like she wanted to say something but refilled her mug instead. "Will you be in the office today?"

"I think I'll inventory the blue room."

"Oh, I wish you luck. I'll help once I'm finished looking at the grocer's bill." At Ava's silence she added, "I'm trying to see if I have enough from the Tiffany lamp to start paying it off."

"That's a smart idea."

"I do have them from time to time." She nudged Ava's arm playfully as she wandered back toward her office.

That afternoon, Ava had finished writing the last bottle ship's name on her notepad—the S.S. *Mauritania*—and was replacing it on the shelf when the spine of a book caught her eye. It was, of course, blue, but something about the ornate gold trim was familiar. It was tucked against a seahorse bookend in the corner, almost as if whoever placed it there was trying to keep it from drawing attention.

Taking it down, she found it wasn't a book but a photo album. The first pages were of a young Harriet, most featuring her childhood, her wearing frilly gowns while posing in various European cities. One looked positively Victorian, with a maybe eleven-year-old Harriet holding a parasol in a matching dress. Her mother and father stood behind her, each looking stone-faced with a hand on their only daughter's shoulders.

She shook her head. How completely different their upbringings had been. Ava recalled one day in November at their first year at Briarcliff, when she'd learned who Harriet Browning was to the New York social scene.

"Pack that marigold dress, Ava," Harriet had said after inviting her to Thanksgiving dinner in Manhattan.

"That one? It's too formal. Who are we dining with, the King of England?"

"No, but the Duke of York's cousin lives in Maine and will be there with his wife."

Ava had nearly dropped her suitcase on her foot. "I can't tell if you're serious."

"Oh, I am," Harriet had replied cheerily, gathering her own clothes. She'd proceeded to state the guest list, leaving Ava bewildered by names she'd only heard about in the papers. She had no idea she'd fallen for one of the most prominent socialites in the northern United States.

"I suppose we did have our good times," she said, laughing at a photo from school: she and Harriet in Charlie Chaplin garb for a talent show performance.

She turned the page, but the edge of another photo poking

out from behind the Chaplin one made her pause. Carefully, she pulled it out.

It was from the 1931 Christmas party at school, right before vacation. Ava hadn't known anyone had taken a photograph of them. Like the others from Harriet's time at school, it was an autochrome. Splashes of color stood out against the darker background where she leaned upon the edge of a green sofa with Harriet. They were both laughing, Ava with her head thrown back, Harriet with one hand over her mouth, her eyes closed in amusement.

They looked young.

They looked happy.

"Ava?"

She spun around to find Harriet in the doorway. Her gaze fell to the album Ava quickly shut.

"Mother put that in here. 'It goes with the room,'" she said in a flittering tone, imitating her mother.

Ava's pulse beat rapidly. She tried to replace the album, but Harriet grabbed it, flipping through it. "I haven't looked at this in ages." She chuckled, commenting on each picture. Meanwhile, Ava kept the photo she'd found in her left hand against her hip and out of sight. "Goodness, can you believe Mother dressed me in that hat? I look absolutely medieval."

Ava snickered, but the photograph in her hand seemed to singe her fingers, shooting a white burst of heat through her arm and into her chest. *We were happy* echoed around her. Her heart seemed to beat too fast, and deep in her mind, an old key turned a lock.

"My, that was a stroll down memory lane. That Chaplin routine was a smash, remember?" Harriet's bright gaze found hers, but Ava couldn't speak. A line creased between Harriet's brows. "Ava?"

She held out the photo.

Harriet took it. A sea of emotions crossed her face. Ava saw the initial surprise followed by an old look she knew well, then guilt. She asked quietly, "This was in there?"

"Behind the Chaplin photo."

Harriet nodded, looking back down, seeming to study the moment from their past.

Finally, Ava found her words. "Why do you have that?"

Harriet's blue eyes shined with an answer. She started to speak, then closed her mouth, shaking her head.

Ava's chest felt full. There was a stirring in her stomach she decided not to fight, and it took over her body. She stepped closer, taking back the photo.

"I tried to forget," Harriet finally said, her eyes low, her voice barely a whisper. "I tried every day, but..." The look in her eyes when her gaze lifted reached into Ava. It ran along the scarred lines of her heart, and to her surprise, the sensation was welcome.

After pocketing the photo, Ava reached out. She ran her fingers from Harriet's temple to her chin as the box inside her mind slowly opened.

Harriet spoke again. "It turns out, Ava Clark, you are impossible to forget."

Flooded with long-quieted feelings, Ava let the tidal wave carry her forward. She pressed her lips to Harriet's. Harriet gave a small gasp but leaned in, letting Ava pull her close. She kissed her back gently, almost timidly. A tremor ran down Ava's spine as their lips moved slowly. She found Harriet's waist, reaching higher, feeling Harriet's supple back beneath her dress. She wrapped one hand around the back of Harriet's neck, pulling her closer, kissing her deeper.

Ava had no idea how long they stood in one another's

embrace, rekindling a fire she thought had long been extinguished. She tugged at Harriet's bottom lip with her teeth. The moan it elicited sent a surge of longing through her.

"Wait," Harriet said, breathless and placing a hand on Ava's sternum.

It took Ava a minute to not focus on Harriet's lips and the way her chest rose and fell.

"Ava, what are we doing?"

She reached up, brushing her knuckles over the smoothness of Harriet's cheek. She'd forgotten how deliciously soft she was. She imagined kissing her again, then reaching out to loosen her bun, running her fingers through Harriet's brown tresses.

Harriet was still talking. "We should...I mean, we shouldn't...that is to say, we ought to talk about this, us, first."

The wave of desire crashed at her feet, and Ava blinked as a sense of lucidity broke through her thoughts. She stepped back, the reality of what she'd just done hitting her like a train. "Talk. Right." God, what had she done? She'd just kissed Harriet Browning. She swore she'd never do that again, ever.

"Never say never," James used to say. She felt mildly dizzy and found the desk to steady herself.

Harriet seemed equally out of sorts. She nodded, muttered something under her breath, then scurried from the room.

Ava stared at the spot where they'd stood moments before. She rubbed her forehead, then scraped her hand down her face. She'd let her emotions get the better of her. She'd let old feelings dictate her actions, something she'd spent fifteen years telling herself not to do.

She closed her eyes, trying to find the collected headspace in which she normally resided. The space where she was calm, put-together, and not in love with Harriet.

She pursed her lips. She could still taste her, feel Harriet's tongue against her own. Ava ran a finger across her lip. *That was not supposed to happen.* More than that, she was not supposed to enjoy it. Because, she realized, taking a shaky breath, she absolutely had.

CHAPTER NINETEEN

Harriet's right leg bounced where she stood, her body trilling with the aftermath of Ava's kiss not minutes before. She clutched the receiver of the office phone to her ear. Finally, the operator connected her.

"H, darling, I'm in the middle of a tea with that scrumptious little blonde from dinner."

"Scar—"

"One moment, the other line is ringing." In a muffled voice, she called, "Imogene, be a dear and grab that. Yes, you may take a message." Clearer, she said, "Positively delightful. She was just telling me about her son's dental fiasco. You wouldn't believe—"

"Scar, we kissed."

Silence, followed by rustling. Harriet imagined Scarlett gathering the phone line, balancing the receiver between her ear and shoulder as she carried the phone to a private corner of the room. "Harriet, tell me everything."

She did, only pausing long enough to catch her breath.

"Oh, sweetheart. I'm thrilled for you."

"What does this mean?" Harriet's chest was embattled, happiness and wariness vying for the space around her heart.

"I know you Northerners do things differently, dear, but

I was under the impression a kiss is one of those universal things."

"We were reminiscing. What if she only got caught up?" Harriet winced, loosening the tight strands of hair on the side of her head. She tried to keep them behind her ear, but like her resolve, it was growing more difficult to maintain.

"Dear, if you're unsure, you need to talk to her."

"What if she says it was a mistake?"

Scarlett was quiet a moment. "You won't know unless you ask, dear."

Sighing, Harriet leaned her head back. Scarlett spoke to someone, then gave a gleeful gasp. "What?"

"H, talk to her. Trust me. She's waiting."

"She's waiting?" But Scarlett hung up. Harriet stared at the receiver, replaying the kiss once again. Harriet would be lying if she said she hadn't dreamt of such a moment ever since she'd left school. She'd survived off those dreams for a long time, determined to be satisfied with fantasies. Could she do that again now that she'd had a taste of the real thing after so long?

She walked to the blue room. The door was cracked. When she pushed it open, Ava wasn't there. She heard the icebox open in the kitchen and found Ava with a bowl of leftover custard on the counter and a spoon in her other hand as she hung up the kitchen telephone.

When she noticed Harriet, she spoke through a healthy heap of custard. "I hope you don't mind. I made a call."

Harriet began to understand Scarlett's comment. "You called Imogene?"

Ava nodded, focusing on another scoop. "Joe answered. Told me she wasn't home. So I tried—"

"Scarlett's?" Harriet joined her, reaching for the custard.

Offering the spoon, Ava frowned. "How did you know?"

"We had the same idea."

Recognition flickered over her face, and Ava smiled. "Of course we did." Taking the dessert back, she asked, "What did Scarlett say?"

"She said I should talk to you as quickly as possible."

Snorting, Ava scooped out more custard.

"Imogene?"

After a satisfied lick of her lips, Ava studied the half-empty bowl. "She said I never should have moved in." The words hit Harriet sharply, not unlike the cold of the custard against the roof of her mouth. It shot through her, a pulse of discomfort across her mind. "Though I don't think she really ever wanted me to take this job."

Harriet found a napkin to dab her mouth clean. "I see." Facing the sink, she said, "I suppose that's fair, after everything." She felt Ava's gaze on her before she replaced the custard and put the spoon in the sink. "Why did you take this job?" she finally asked.

Ava faced her. They stood five paces apart, Harriet with her back to the sink. When she didn't say anything for a time, Harriet spoke:

"After graduation, I never thought I would see you again. I hoped I would, but I had this awful feeling deep in my bones that you were gone from my life."

The muscle along Ava's jaw tightened.

"I can't imagine the pain I caused you. If it was half as terrible as how I felt—"

"How *you* felt?" Ava's voice had a hard edge. "Harriet, you betrayed me. You betrayed *us*."

Harriet felt the need to run writhe in her gut, but she forced herself to face Ava. "I know. I know I did." She started to explain herself, but Ava already knew her reasons for doing what she had. Harriet hadn't been able to fathom a path in life without a man's title and money. It had taken her years to realize how fickle all of that was, how ultimately, she was the only one who could control her own happiness.

Ava stepped closer. "I told myself I'd never think of you again. I'd never see your face in the paper, never hear your name. I pushed all of it away, kept it under lock and key." With one hand, she pushed at the air as if once again trying to shove what they had aside. Harriet's chest felt ready to burst at the description of her own attempts to move on after college.

Now only two steps away, Ava's brown eyes shone. "I told myself I'd never want you again."

"Ava, I can't undo what happened. But I can't tell you how happy I was to see you when you showed up for that interview."

Ava seemed to search her gaze. Harriet longed to pull her close, but she didn't want to push this. The kiss had been blissful, but if it was to be the only one, so be it. She still struggled to believe anyone, especially Ava, could want her like this: a dwindling reputation, financial straits, and a burgeoning reclusive nature. Losing Ava again was unthinkable. She refused to be responsible for the break of their bonds a second time. Harriet would fight to keep Ava in her life, even if it was only as a friend.

"I didn't expect my time here to go the way it has." Ava squinted, her head tilting slightly. "You're different."

Harriet reached up, self-conscious about the loose strands around her face.

She continued. "I didn't realize what you were going through."

Harriet met her gaze. "We've both had our times."

She shook her head, then stepped closer. Reaching up, she

gently ran her thumb across Harriet's cheek. "I should have known."

"What?" asked Harriet, reaching to take her hand.

She smiled. "Things rarely go the way I plan." Then she cupped Harriet's face.

Only a breath apart, Harriet closed her eyes. The resolve she was clinging to unraveled at Ava's closeness. She leaned in, but Ava pulled back. Harriet grinned at the familiar, teasing gesture. "Ava."

"Yes?"

She gripped Ava's waist. "I'm dying to kiss you again."

"Are you?"

A low heat stirred below her stomach, and Harriet dug her fingers into Ava's hips at being denied what she wanted. "I am."

"What else are you dying to do?"

A moan escaped her lips, and she reached for Ava's neck. She tried to pull her closer, but Ava held her ground, a sly grin below her dark eyes. It took Harriet a moment, but she managed to collect herself enough to pull Ava's gaze. She leaned next to her ear and thrilled at the way Ava's breath caught when she whispered, "Let me show you."

Harriet led her into the guest room. It had taken extreme willpower not to push her against the counter, onto the kitchen table, or up against the wall. She knew, though, this had to be slow. She wanted this to last, and she was determined to make every moment count.

Evening light fell through the curtains, creating a soft glow. Instinctively, Harriet went to close the door, then remembered she didn't have to. Seeming to sense her thoughts, Ava gave a knowing smile.

The bed was made, and Harriet guided her to it. They still hadn't said a word, but Harriet could feel the tension between them. She could see Ava's wants in the corner of her smile, in her brown eyes watching, waiting.

Harriet ran her hands from Ava's shoulders to the cuffs of her blouse. It was outrageous, really, how good she looked in a button-down. Harriet let herself stare at Ava's bosom, her waist, taking her in, etching this Ava into her mind.

When Ava stepped forward, Harriet pushed her back, forcing her to sit at the foot of the bed. Their fingers intertwined; Harriet looked into eyes that begged her to touch. Harriet would, but two could play the teasing game.

Straddling her, Harriet drew Ava's arms behind her, closer to the bed, keeping them behind her back. A faint groan told Harriet this was going to be fun. She kissed the pulse point on Ava's neck, trailing kisses up to her ear. A gentle bite elicited a sharp breath, and Ava bucked. Harriet laughed, kissing down her jaw. Then she found Ava's lips. This kiss wasn't like the one in the blue room. It was deeper, fiercer. Ava pushed forward. Harriet kept Ava's arms pinned, keeping control as she pressed herself against Ava's hips.

Ava managed to work one hand free, finding Harriet's back. For a moment, Harriet let her hold on as they kissed, arousal surging from her core, filling the space between her legs. When Ava squeezed her hip, then moved, Harriet caught her hand. "Not yet."

Ava groaned in protest. Harriet stood, her breath coming fast as Ava reached for her. Harriet grabbed her hands, clutching them. She kissed Ava's knuckles. God, how she'd missed this. She kissed her again, then lowered her gaze to the button on Ava's trousers. Her shoes already kicked off, Ava quickly undid her pants and slipped them off. Harriet leaned down, her hands on top of Ava's bare thighs. "Spread your legs."

Ava did. Harriet bit her lip at the sight of Ava's underwear already wet with desire. Kneeling, she kissed her over the soft fabric. Another gasp and Ava scooted closer.

Holding Ava's gaze, Harriet pulled the underwear off, tossing them aside. "You're so beautiful." She kissed up Ava's left thigh, then across the patch of trimmed hair at her center, down her other thigh. A kiss to Ava's swollen clit prompted a deep moan.

Harriet stood, and Ava lifted her head. Yearning and lust mingled in her dark gaze. Slowly, Harriet unbuttoned Ava's blouse, leaving kisses along the top of her breasts. When Ava reached back, undoing the clasp to her bra, Harriet grinned. "I remember you being more patient."

Ava pulled her down into a fiery kiss. Desire raced from her lips to her core, and Harriet quickly knelt again. The moment she took Ava in her mouth, Ava cried out. Her hand came up to the back of Harriet's head, bringing her closer. Harriet licked slowly at first, relishing the way Ava tasted. She felt her own desire grow slick between her legs but focused on Ava spread open before her. Each stroke prompted a gasp, a moan, some beautiful sound from Ava, who leaned back, still with one hand keeping Harriet in place.

Another flick of the tongue against Ava's clit made her buck, and Harriet couldn't stop her own moan from escaping as Ava said hoarsely, "Harriet, don't stop."

Harriet wouldn't have dreamed of doing such a thing. She let Ava hold her there as she tasted her, took her, until a short series of moans from Ava turned into a single, emphatic cry. Beneath her, Ava trembled, and Harriet gave one final, loving stroke.

The room had seemed to expand at Ava's cries, the walls shuddering with their own breaths. Now, it slowly realigned itself in their aftermath. Eventually, Ava released her. Harriet leaned back. Using the base of her wrist, she wiped Ava from her chin, licking her lips clean. Her center throbbed with the need for release, but she only moved to kneel on one knee, watching Ava regain her breath.

When Ava finally sat up, her face flushed, she wore a look Harriet couldn't quite read. Her cheeks were pink, her chest still rising and falling quickly. Her eyes were no longer clouded with ardent desire but still looked at Harriet in a way that made her shiver. There was something else in them, too. Something Harriet hadn't seen in more than fifteen years.

Her heart pounded as Ava reached to cup her face. She was completely overwhelmed with a sensation of something warm sweeping across her heart. Simultaneously, she was utterly dazed with lust and longing. Harriet closed her eyes, turning to kiss Ava's palm. Emotions danced through her chest, leaping into her throat and nearly escaping from her tongue. "Ava…"

Ava's forefinger found her lips, pressing against them to quiet her. "Hush now. It's my turn."

CHAPTER TWENTY

Ava had no idea what time it was when she woke. Harriet's left arm was across her waist, holding tight while she lay flush against her. On her back, Ava turned, placing a kiss on Harriet's forehead while she slept.

The room was dark. Several pillows and the plush comforter had fallen to the floor. Ava and Harriet lay tangled amid the cream-colored sheet as Ava gently brushed back strands from Harriet's face.

She felt blissfully tired, the kind of tired she hadn't felt in some time. Her body hummed, content. She replayed their moments together: Harriet surprising her with her forwardness, Ava reciprocating with equal passion, Harriet's cries of pleasure when Ava had touched her.

Harriet muttered something in her sleep. Ava pulled her closer. Being together had felt like when they were younger. Something was different, though. They still knew how to touch each other, but Harriet had showed a new confidence. In school, it had been Ava leading them most nights, rushing to a climax before one of their roommates returned, or someone suspected they had disappeared too long from a party.

Tonight, Harriet had taken every moment slowly, ensuring each kiss, each movement, lasted. It had been the way Ava had always dreamed of for them. Finally, they'd had the freedom Ava used to long for. They'd made love without any concerns save for one another.

Ava swallowed. *Made love.* Was that what they'd done? Her heart continued its quick beating, a new fullness in her chest. Looking into Harriet's eyes as they'd been together had sent her to a place that had long lived behind a veil in her mind. Since starting work, she had recognized the old tension between them. She'd tried to ignore it, determined to be above her former feelings. Giving into her distant wants had seemed foolish, weak. But getting to know Harriet again, being around her once more, was new in a way she hadn't expected. It was easy, lighthearted, yet their conversations broached topics they'd never spoken of in school. They were open in a way they'd never been. Ava smiled. Could she really be falling for Harriet all over again?

It was just after dawn when she heard the curtains being opened. Harriet had donned her silk slip and stood by the window in the early morning light. "Good morning."

Ava was on her stomach, hands beneath her pillow when she turned. "Morning."

Harriet placed a kiss on Ava's temple. Sitting beside her, she ran her fingers up and down Ava's arm as she spoke. "I'll make us some coffee." She hesitated. "How are you feeling?"

Ava replied, "Fine."

Harriet pursed her lips. "I mean, about last night."

Ava knew that was what she'd meant but couldn't seem to pinpoint how exactly she was feeling. Happy, confused, satisfied. "A bit hungry after everything," she decided to go with, laying on a smile for good measure before kissing Harriet's knuckles.

Harriet searched her gaze. Ava knew she wanted to talk about it, but where would that conversation lead? Feelings had sparked anew in Ava, but the memory of Harriet abandoning her—abandoning them—all those years ago was still as vivid as the day it had happened. She couldn't possibly lay her heart out a second time only for Harriet to reject her once again. The distant possibility of hope for the two of them was daunting.

Ava turned onto her side. She traced the skin on Harriet's thigh, lifting the hem of her slip. There was, she reasoned, no harm in having a little more fun, something to quell the tidal wave of thoughts raging in her mind. "Why don't we wait a bit on the coffee?"

Harriet arched a brow. "I thought you were hungry?"

"I am."

Grinning, Harriet leaned down, and Ava kissed her, pulling her back to bed.

At ten, they finally managed to tear themselves away from each other. Ava made them eggs and toast. They sipped coffee in the kitchen while Ava made sure to steer the conversation away from the night before, focusing instead on their plans for the auction.

"You're sure you want to invite everyone?" she asked.

Harriet took another bite of breakfast. "I think so. Why not? Once the advertisement goes out, everyone will know anyway. I might as well go out in style with formal invitations." They spent the next half hour discussing invitees, and Ava had to admit she got a kick out of recalling some of the quirky members of New York's elite. "I can't believe Aaron Post insisted on the same cat four times in a row. They really named each one Reginald?"

"They really did. Not even a Reginald the Second or Third. Each one was simply Reginald."

"Some people really have trouble moving on."

"I've never had a pet, but I imagine it would be hard to let go."

Ava laughed. "Perhaps." She scanned the list they'd jotted down on a notepad. "The Forbeses and Astors?"

"Yes, keep them on the list. But I don't think the Smiths will attend. They've been a bit on the outskirts of things. Jacob moved to Europe to put distance between himself and the scandal of his affair." She named a few other families who had fallen on hard times since the 1930s. "The Depression and the Great Wars certainly changed the fabric of things," she mused, leaning back in her seat.

Ava nodded. "'Evened the playing field,' so Imogene says."

Harriet snorted, but a sad glint filled her eyes. Ava chewed her cheek. She'd never fully understood the way a lot of the American aristocracy acted. People with everything had a strange way of knowing very little about the world. Still, Harriet was right in that society had changed over the last fifteen years. The middle-class was growing, and people like the Astors, Kelloggs, and even Harriet Browning had been forced a few steps closer to everyone else.

They spent another hour debating ink type for the invitations, along with color schemes, eventually landing on a classic black and gold combination. It was already August fifth. Invitations would go out in a week's time, leaving three weeks for RSVPs before the event on September tenth.

"We should finish inventorying by next weekend, too. I'll call Monday to schedule the appraiser."

Ava nodded, turning her mug on the table. Harriet reached out, resting her hand on Ava's. "What is it?"

Ava met her gaze. She'd been thinking about their time together. The time they had left. There was only a month before this apartment would be cleared out, and Harriet would be forced to move. They hadn't talked more about where she might end up; Ava had a feeling Harriet was dreading the decision. And if Ava dared to dwell in that scarred place near her heart, she was dreading it, too.

That was why it was better not to say anything about last night, Ava told herself. She watched Harriet, who gathered their dishes and took them to the sink. It was too dangerous to completely let down her walls again. Not only was there a very good chance of Harriet being unwilling to commit, but they only had borrowed time left. She kept forgetting she was here to do a job, even if those lines had blurred last night. Harriet might be single now, but what would make her want to be with Ava when she had a dwindling business empire to try to salvage, and Ava...well, Ava barely had rent money? Part of her knew that Harriet had never cared about her social status or how much money she had. Still, she hesitated, knowing that when all of this began, they'd agreed to certain terms. Ava was here until September, and that was it. Ultimately, it was easier to ride it out, though she'd have to leave Harriet again. At least this time, it would be on her terms.

She realized she hadn't answered when Harriet glanced over her shoulder and said, "Ava?"

"Just going over logistics. We've got our work cut out for us this week."

Harriet smiled. "Nothing we can't handle." She left their mugs and dried her hands. Crossing the room, she added, "Besides, today's Sunday." She pulled Ava to stand. "That's business for Monday."

Ava's heart had been battling the swirl of emotions in her chest. She couldn't help but laugh, though, as Harriet led her back to the bedroom.

CHAPTER TWENTY-ONE

Monday and Tuesday went by too fast. Harriet and Ava started work at nine each morning after breakfast and kept their noses to their inventory lists until sundown, only breaking for a short lunch of cheese sandwiches and milk. Harriet blinked, stretching each night, surprised how the day vanished behind them like the sun behind the towering offices outside. She hated how quickly time was passing. The only good thing was that the nights also came fast, nights spent in Ava's arms. They didn't talk about it, only fell into a routine of light dinners, cool baths, then crawling into bed together.

Harriet held on to their moments each night, relished each touch, every breath that passed between their lips. She hoped Ava knew what she was growing more certain of each day: how blissful it was to be together again.

Still, she didn't broach the topic when the sun rose each morning. Something in Ava's gaze was guarded, despite her unabashed cries in the night, and Harriet couldn't bring herself to push a conversation.

Instead, Harriet poured her frazzled thoughts and energy into planning the auction. The appraiser would come next week to price the majority of her possessions. They'd compiled what remained of her parents' art in the library. Meanwhile, her father's books were arranged throughout the office, and the other fine decorative pieces were scattered across every surface of the blue room and main living room.

"I'll be back," Ava called from the office doorway on Wednesday at midday.

Harriet looked up from the invitation she was signing. Her hand ached from writing thirty since this morning, and she replaced her fountain pen to stretch her fingers. "You're leaving?" A feeling like she'd missed a step sank her stomach to the floor.

One hand on the doorjamb, a small smile lifted Ava's lips. "Your dry cleaning is ready."

"Oh, right." She waved and listened to the elevator as Ava left. She sat back. Each time Ava ran an errand lately, Harriet had a sinking feeling that she might not return. What if she regretted what was transpiring between them?

Harriet stared at the empty doorway. Envisioning Ava standing there, she smiled at the beautiful phantom Ava had been for more than a decade. Someone she'd thought about every day for years. She'd envisioned her so often, she had sometimes appeared among the crowd at a charity event, seated in the corner of a café, in a theatre, or in Harriet's bed. Now the real Ava had appeared in her life again. At first, Harriet had been certain the occurrence would unravel her, drop her to her knees at the reality of the woman she'd always loved having finally returned.

That was how it had been for Harriet when they were younger: a deep, aching need for Ava, for her company, her laugh, her touch. She frowned, realizing it wasn't that she needed Ava now. Yes, when it came to her job, Ava was helpful and a joy to be around. But it wasn't an ardent ache that filled Harriet like it had at school. Their time at Briarcliff had felt like a flash of frantic longings compressed into hidden moments.

Each one of those moments was intensified by the hot flicker of desire, of urgent needs that had to be met.

Now, it was different. Perhaps because she knew it would end. But that sharp requirement was gone. She sat back in her chair as the knowledge dawned on her that she hadn't actually needed Ava, or anyone, really, for a long time. Save for the last few months, she'd handled things on her own. So, no, she didn't need Ava anymore. She wanted her.

She wanted Ava more than anything. Wanted her in her life. But could Ava want her, too? What if the auction didn't leave her with enough money? Harriet imagined asking Ava to join her when all of this was said and done, but with the caveat that she had a job. She hated the idea of forcing Ava to work just for them to be together while Harriet tried to sort things out with her father's mills. Ava was a working woman, but what if she resented Harriet for not being able to provide for them? Part of her knew Ava wouldn't care about such things, but a life with no security was new and left Harriet doubting.

Nearly an hour later, the elevator sounded, and footsteps hurried down the hall. "Ava, I'm still in here," Harriet called, signing another invitation and wondering how much her father's Kipling first editions might go for.

"Sorry to disappoint, darling." Scarlett flounced through the doorway in a pair of sleek trousers and a blouse accented with ruffles down the front.

"Scar, what are you doing here?" Noticing a large casserole dish in her hands, Harriet pointed, "Is that...did you bake?"

She pouted, placing the dish carefully atop the coffee table before dropping her hat and matching handbag onto the sofa. "I made what my cook calls a Lime Delight Cake. We had it at last week's dinner for Paul's business meeting, and it was a smash. You haven't called in a few days, so I thought, nothing like a sweet to help with stress." Scarlett beamed before plopping down beside her things on the sofa. At Harriet's confused look, she added, "I know I'm not a well-endowed, brown-eyed blonde, but really, H, I'm offended."

Harriet grimaced. "I'm sorry. Really, thank you for the cake," she added sincerely. Scarlett straightened, giving an accepting nod. "It's been"—she rubbed a finger against her temple—"a lot, lately."

Scarlett's gaze swept over the stacks of books that littered the room, seeming to pause at Ava's jacket on the back of a chair and Harriet's loose bun. "So I see."

"We're planning the auction, and I'm trying to finish these invitations before Saturday." She tried fruitlessly to suppress a blush at Scarlett's knowing look that planning the auction wasn't the only thing she and Ava had been doing. Clearing her throat, she tried to push stray hairs back into her bun.

Scarlett found a finished stack on the coffee table. "September tenth." Her mischievous smile spread. "Only a week after the McCarthy benefit? H, you minx. Nobody's dared to schedule within two weeks of a McCarthy event for the last twenty years. Not since that poor woman…I forget her name, and that was probably Martha's doing, back in '28."

"You weren't even living here in '28."

"That's precisely my point! It's legendary."

Harriet shook her head. "I don't have a choice. Everything needs to be gone by then. That date gives us a couple weeks to ship things and pack the rest up." Scarlett's eyebrows had raised at both instances of Harriet saying "we" and "us." She gave a small shrug, knowing Scarlett could read the silent acknowledgment of the truth behind Harriet's words. The truth of Ava being a part of her life again. "Do you think Martha will have a fit when she gets her invitation?"

Scarlett nodded. "The woman can't help it. She thrives off scheduling scandals." At Harriet's sigh, she added, "Don't worry, I'll break the news to some of the gals at tea tomorrow so they're prepared. Martha McCarthy's only one woman, after all."

One woman with powerful opinions, Harriet thought, but bit her tongue. At her silence, Scarlett asked, "Where is the magnificent Ava? I'd hoped to see her."

"She's out. Running an errand." She glanced at the clock.

Following her gaze, Scarlett asked, "What is it?"

"It's nothing." She waved a hand. "Just me being silly."

"Nonsense."

"It's just…" She sat forward, bringing her elbows to rest atop the desk. "Each time Ava leaves, I'm afraid that's it. She'll take the elevator down and never return."

Scarlett studied her. "Why would she do that?"

"Because we—" She cut herself off, the words catching in her throat. Scarlett gave a sympathetic frown, patting the cushion next to her. Harriet stood and joined her. "It's been absolutely wonderful since we…" She felt a blush fill her cheeks. "Well, since we reunited. Each time is incredible, better than the last."

Whistling, Scarlett fanned herself, her drawl exaggerated. "H, darling, please."

Harriet laughed. "I'm sorry." She shook her head. "I hope she can feel how much I want this. How much I want her. But we haven't talked about it."

"About where you'll go next?"

"About any of it. Everything is as it was when she started. We agreed on a timeline. Once September ends, she'll be done here, and I'll be gone."

Scarlett quirked her lips upward, her bright red lipstick scrunched. Eventually, she said, "It sounds like an important conversation ought to be had soon."

Harriet clenched her jaw, frustrated as she pictured

Ava's smile falter or her shoulder turning away when their conversations fell quiet. "I know. Each time I get close to talking to her, her eyes change, like she can sense what I'm going to say. Those walls of hers go up, and she guards her heart from me."

Scarlett reached out, resting a hand on hers. Softly, she said, "I don't blame her for that, darling."

Sighing, Harriet said, "I know. Neither do I."

"Give her time."

"We're running out of that, Scar."

They both fell quiet until Scarlett insisted that they needed tea. They even sliced the cake, both stepping back at how green the spongy dessert was. Still, Harriet was grateful for something to fill the chasm that the lack of Ava's presence left in her apartment. Upon returning from the kitchen with a tray, Harriet picked up her saucer but struggled to keep her cup even atop it.

"H, you're trembling. Whatever is the matter?"

The color of the tea with milk reminded her of the flecks of light brown in Ava's eyes. She closed her own, taking a deep breath. "I'm afraid."

"Of what? Hurting Ava?" Scarlett took a sip, then said gently, "I hate to break it to you, H, but that ship has sailed."

"I wouldn't do that to her again."

"Then tell her that."

Harriet set her cup and saucer on the table. "Scar."

She gave a sigh. "H, I won't lie to you." She took another sip, then placed her cup beside Harriet's. "I was angry with you when you divorced my brother." Her words hit like a bee sting, quick and sharp, but Scarlett continued. "I wasn't angry because you weren't going to be together anymore. I was afraid of losing you as my sister."

Harriet didn't know what to say. She'd been taken with

Scarlett when they'd first met at her engagement party fifteen years ago. She recalled thinking that even if she had to marry Lawrence, at least his sister was somebody whose company she would enjoy. The memories of heated conversations with Lawrence over the dinner table, a harshly lit lawyer's office, then breaking the news to her own parents that they were divorcing rushed back. She'd been certain all of the Atkins clan would shun her.

Harriet quirked her head. "Is that why you were suddenly so busy right after everything? It seemed every time I called, you were with Lawrence."

Scarlett nodded. "I told myself that if I was to lose you as my sister, I ought to just get it over with. I'm Lawrence's family, after all. Tradition dictated I side with him." Harriet raised her brow, and Scarlett answered her silent question. "I know. We're twentieth century women, to hell with tradition. I realized that eventually, thank goodness."

After a minute, Harriet said, "I didn't mean to hurt Lawrence or you."

"Of course you didn't. But, H, don't you realize that was your first big step? That was you breaking away from the chains of this silly world's weight placed upon your shoulders. That was you being brave. God knows, that's not easy in this life, especially for us." She smiled, taking Harriet's hands in her gloved ones. "Divorcing my brother was the first step to you becoming this woman. This woman who has handled herself magnificently amid complete chaos and uncertainty for the last decade." Scarlett's eyes watered, and Harriet felt tears on her cheeks. "That is a woman I'm proud to call my friend."

Harriet held Scarlett's gaze, taking in her words, trying to believe them. Could she really be that woman? Could she be brave? She'd given in to so much fear when she was younger; fear of letting people down, of not fitting in to the life she'd known, of being different. But by succumbing to the expectations of herself, her family, and the perpetually omnipresent members of her social circle, she'd let down the person she cared about most, digging a crater in her heart that only now seemed to be closing.

"It'll work out," Scarlett was saying. "My former sister-in-law is Harriet Browning, strong, smart, and even if she doesn't know it, brave."

Harriet wiped at the tears on her cheeks. "I don't know what I did to deserve you, Scar." She gripped her hands tightly. "You're a gem, you know that?"

They hugged. Over her shoulder, Scarlett said, "Gems attract light, darling. Yours has never been brighter."

Sitting back, Harriet smiled. Ava was the reason for that rediscovered light. Scarlett was right. There were no more family members to tell her what to do. The prying eyes and gossiping mouths waiting in the wings seemed like mere shadows. There was no one left to hold her back but herself.

After they finished their tea, Harriet said good-bye to Scarlett, promising she would try to be brave. She hadn't backed down from the turmoil of her family's financial crisis or her father's unexpected death or the slow demise of the Browning empire. She'd be damned if she backed down from a second chance at a life with Ava Clark.

Chapter Twenty-Two

There was much for the appraiser to do when he returned the following Tuesday morning to finish the job. He greeted them both cordially enough, his hand sweaty when Ava shook it. A middle-age man with black hair that ran from ear to ear across the back of his head, his watery eyes bugged a little less at Harriet's extravagant possessions the second day as compared to the first. He moved meticulously through the apartment, occasional hushed gasps escaping his puckered mouth in between mutterings as he made notes on his clipboard.

Ava stayed out of the way as Harriet finished the last batch of auction invitations. She decided to run back to her apartment after lunch. Dusting would be a good idea; she didn't want to return in a month to more cobwebs than usual.

Taking the train back to Brooklyn didn't hold the same verve it once had. The constant movement of city life was now a grating monotone compared to the peaceful quiet of Harriet's apartment. Ava laughed, wondering if she'd managed to become spoiled from such a short time in upper Manhattan. Perhaps, she thought. The soft carpet, the thick curtains, and Harriet's touch had unknowingly become staples. The harsh smells and sounds that berated her senses now overwhelmed her. As the train rambled on, Ava lost herself in dreams of

Harriet and the feeling of falling into her arms the last few nights.

As she took the stairs to her apartment building, Ava conjured the image of Harriet beneath her. She bit her lip as she replayed placing kisses down her body. It was so good with Harriet. Each day together soothed Ava's heart like a balm she hadn't even known she'd needed. The same calming notion spiked trepidation, though. How could she be sure of what Harriet truly wanted? She'd been a secret before in Harriet's life and wouldn't be so again. The new earnestness in Harriet's touch, the openness of their conversations, was promising. Still, Ava feared letting herself fall fully for Harriet again. It would only lead to the scars on her heart tearing open, and this time, the damage would be irreparable.

In her apartment, she opened the window to her fire escape to air things out. She ran a rag over the counter when there was a knock on the door.

"Mr. Wakowski," she greeted him and stepped aside, but he didn't move to come in. Instead, he pulled a piece of mail from his robe pocket. When he didn't say anything, she took it. "Thanks. How were the lemon bars?"

"Fine." He looked past her into the apartment, then down at her feet, perhaps searching for a suitcase.

"I'm just straightening up," she said. "I'm still at my other residence until the end of September. Which reminds me." She left the door ajar and fetched her handbag. "Here's next month's rent in advance. I know my lease is up in October, but I'll be back by then to discuss things."

He nodded, then met her gaze. The expectant look he wore made Ava wonder if he hoped for more lemon bars. When she only smiled, glancing at her mail, he turned and left. Closing the door, Ava sifted through it at her kitchen table. She paused at the familiar United States Navy logo. Swallowing, she held it carefully, framing it with both hands. Taking a shaky breath, she opened it.

Miss Clark,

After further investigation and the complete exhaustion of our available resources, we regret to inform you that Private James Henry Clark remains classified as Missing in Action, supposed drowned, as of May 1944. We have decided to close your brother's file.

Private J. H. Clark upheld the noble traditions of the American Navy. We hope this realization may soften the blow of this decision. We thank you and your family for your commitment to our country.

She fell into the chair. Rereading the letter, Ava stared so hard that the black ink blurred. It took her a moment to realize it was tears obstructing her vision. The letter still in one hand, she fell forward onto the table, her face hidden in the crook of her elbow as she wept. She wept for her brothers, she wept for the hundreds of soldiers who would never be found, and she wept for her family.

When she regained her breath, Ava set the letter aside. She felt stiff, automatic, as she went into the hall and found the phone.

"I swear, they watch me like a hawk around here. Good thing they pay so well," Imogene huffed. Ava smiled at the sound of her voice. She started to speak but felt a lump rise in her throat. She worked to clear it as Imogene asked, "Ava, are you okay?"

Finally, she managed to say, "I got another letter."

A sound like rustling, followed by Imogene whispering, "And?"

This time, Ava couldn't fight the break in her voice. "I can't do it anymore. They're closing his file. He's not coming back, Imogene. James is gone."

"Oh, Ava."

Imogene sat quietly on the other end while Ava let herself cry. "Missing doesn't mean dead," she heard in her mind. The mantra she'd held on to for so long. Only now did she understand how she'd been in that same place, hanging on to the edge of yesterday. Always looking back to how it was, how things used to be, not how they really were. Missing might not have meant dead, but her brother was gone. Both William and James weren't coming home.

"I'm sorry, hon. Where are you?" Imogene asked.

Ava sniffed. "At my apartment."

"Your apartment?" She caught the surprise in Imogene's voice. "Want me to come over? I'll tell them I had bad mayo for lunch. Wouldn't be the first time."

"No." Ava shook her head, turning her back to Mr. Wakowski's door and clutching the receiver. "I'll be all right. I've got to get back soon, anyway."

"If you're sure." Imogene hesitated a beat. "How is all of that?"

Ava took a breath. "Can something be really good but really scary at the same time?"

"I think that's the basic idea behind carnival rides and horror flicks."

Ava replied, "Harriet and I must be on the world's wildest roller coaster, then." She quickly recounted events from the last week.

"Ava, that's a fine line you're walking with her."

"I know. It's not like it was, though. It's—"

"Different. Yeah, you've said."

Ava winced. She didn't blame Imogene for not being

encouraging when it came to Harriet. Imogene had been there when Ava was the most broken, a hollow shell in the aftermath of Harriet leaving her.

"I understand your concern," she said. "Trust me. I don't want to repeat history."

"Then what's so confusing?"

Ava fiddled with the worn edge of the phone box. How could she explain the grounded, self-assured nature Harriet possessed now? How could she explain the blaze of desire she saw in Harriet's gaze each night, the perfect ease with which they worked together, not just professionally, but in the newfound space that lay somewhere between friends and something more?

"I think I'm falling in love with her again," she whispered, frightened by her own admission.

Imogene was quiet for so long, Ava thought the call might've disconnected. "Does she feel the same?"

"I think so. But—"

"Ava." Imogene cut her off. "Until you can say that sentence without a 'but,' be careful. Do what you have to, but keep that big, beautiful heart of yours at the front of your concerns."

When their call ended, Ava returned to her letters. Mostly bills, save for one. At the bottom of the pile was a letter from her parents. Guilt crept up her neck at another message from them after she still hadn't written back in over a year. She nearly tossed it, unopened, into the drawer next to the others. After closing the window and grabbing her handbag, though, she quickly shoved it into her pocket and took it with her back to Fifth Avenue.

❖

The sound of the elevator sent a rush of relief through Harriet. She smiled, continuing to slice two cheese and cucumber sandwiches as Ava's familiar tread sounded behind her in the kitchen.

"Sorry it took me so long."

"Did it? I hadn't noticed," she replied over her shoulder. Ava's lifted brow said she saw right through that response. Harriet turned back to wrap the food in a napkin before setting it inside an oversized wicker basket. "Everything fine back in Brooklyn?"

"Just fine." Ava stepped closer, picking up a full thermos from the counter. "What's all this?"

"Well, the appraiser won't be done for at least another hour. I thought we'd give him some room."

"Picnicking with Bert in the lobby?"

"I thought we'd walk over to the park."

She wasn't surprised by Ava's slack-jawed silence. Still, Harriet lifted her chin as if she was offended.

"Are you sure?" Ava asked.

She couldn't help but love the concern in her tone. Harriet laughed. "You speak as if I'm doing something scandalous." She used the handle to rest the basket in the crook of her arm. "Well, perhaps I am. There's a bench on the park's edge that's always vacant. It's not far, and it's quiet." Meeting Ava's gaze, she added, "I'd like to try again."

A flash of something lit Ava's eyes. She smiled, then took the basket. "Well, then. After you."

Like the Fourth, Harriet ignored the bombardment of curious eyes following her across the lobby. Unlike that time, she didn't feel the overwhelming sensation that she didn't belong. Not even when they stepped outside.

Scurrying across the busy street, Harriet led them to the bench. It was the same one she'd sat on nearly two months before. Then, she'd felt utterly helpless as she'd floundered in the chaos of her financial woes. The lack of stability and the uncertainty at her own future had sent her into a frenzied state. The simple act of sitting on a bench had been unbearable. There had been too much possibility of being seen, her family's downfall somehow written in the look in her eyes. A single glimpse from a passerby was all it would have taken to finish the collapse of the Browning empire. One look and she would have crumbled. Thus, it had been easier to hide.

Now, she took a deep breath of fresh air as Ava handed her one of the sandwiches after they took a seat. The late afternoon breeze was warm but broke through the heat as the end of summer slowly approached.

"One of these days, I'm gonna show you how to make a PB and J," Ava said, drawing Harriet's gaze away from the skyscrapers.

"A what?"

Ava laughed. "It will change your world."

Harriet smiled. "If you insist." They sat quietly. After pouring tea, Harriet said, "Ava, I don't know if I'll ever be able to properly thank you for all that you've done. Truly. I..." She cleared her throat. "I wasn't in a good place before. You've done so much, and I'm so grateful."

Ava ran her thumb across her bottom lip to swipe at droplets of tea. She seemed to ponder her words. As she started to reply, a high-pitched voice cut through the peaceful air. "Miss Browning, is that really you?"

"Martha." Harriet set her sandwich down. Instinctually, she stood, embracing Martha McCarthy before exchanging air kisses.

"Why, it's been ages, dear, simply ages." Her matronly figure was wrapped in a fetching dress. Layers of necklaces fell below her high neckline while several hefty rings sparkled from her knuckles. Harriet glanced at her own simple dress and flattened her collar. She remembered she hadn't put makeup on today and could feel Martha scrutinizing her plain appearance.

"It's lovely to see you, Martha," Harriet replied. Ava remained seated, watching them over her plastic cup. Harriet glanced sideways, but Martha—who seemed fixated on her— said, "You look incredibly trim, dear. And that complexion of yours is porcelain. Here I thought the young ladies these days were going for a more sunned look." Her laughter trilled down the tree-lined path; several passersby turned their way.

Harriet gave a tight smile. "I haven't had much opportunity this summer to get out."

"What has kept you so busy lately?" Martha leaned forward, and Harriet caught the musky scent of her high-end perfume. "You haven't rekindled things with Lawrence, have you?"

Ava's cough nearly made Harriet laugh. "No. He seems content with his starlets of the week. I haven't checked the socials in a while, but last I saw, it was some leggy European." Martha's eyes widened at her candidness. "I've actually been working on family business, if you must know." From the corner of her eye, she saw Ava's posture shift, no doubt surprised at her admitting such information. Martha's eyebrows, meanwhile, shot skyward, her small mouth puckered at this sliver of gossip.

"Oh? Well, I hope it won't interfere with you attending our benefit Labor Day weekend. It would be so good to see you there." Her words dripped with what Harriet used to believe was haughty sincerity. Perhaps a small part of Martha did want her to attend, but Harriet saw through the caked-on makeup, the flash of jewels that kept catching the late afternoon light, the overenthusiastic tone of voice. She took Harriet's hand, patting it as if she was an aunt trying to dismiss a tiresome niece. Martha still hadn't acknowledged Ava's presence.

An idea struck Harriet. She reached into her pocket. "I'm not sure I'll be able to make it this year. You see, I've got my own event to finish planning." She handed Martha an auction invitation. She'd intended it as scrap paper after some of the ink smudged but realized it, like many other things in her life, no longer needed to be perfect.

"September tenth?" Martha's voice pitched even higher. Her wrinkled fingers shook as she stared at the invitation.

"Yes. The rest of these will be going out in a few days. And the advertisement will go to print Friday. Congratulations on being the first to know about the Browning estate auction." Each word only broadened her smile, and Harriet was astonished at how light she felt.

Martha seemed perplexed as she gaped at the paper. "Miss Browning, you've been away for some time," she started carefully, an edge to her voice when she said, "away." "You may have forgotten that it's typical to consult the event calendar so as not to overwhelm everyone's schedule. Late summer is already frightfully fraught with to-dos." Her gaze was still wide but turned sharp as she lowered her voice. "I urge you to reschedule immediately. This sort of faux-pax would be detrimental to—"

"My reputation?" Harriet finished, and Martha stepped back. "With all respect, there comes a time when there are more important things than overbooking the social pages."

Martha only blinked, one bejeweled hand over her chest in apparent astonishment.

"By the way, say hello to Ava Clark." She motioned for Ava to stand. She did, wearing an amused grin.

Still looking stunned, Martha frowned. "Have we met?"

"Long time ago," Ava said, shaking Martha's hand.

"Ava is my…she's helped me greatly these last couple of months. She's practically organized the auction herself." When Martha only gawked, she added, "I do hope to see you there. That way, you will truly be able to appreciate all the effort Ava's put in. I believe you have my address?"

Martha nodded as Ava added, "Harriet's the true work-horse, Madame McCarthy." She nudged Harriet's shoulder, and they both held back laughs at Martha's bewildered face.

Martha only nodded before bidding them a good evening.

When she was gone, Harriet fell back on the bench in a fit of laughter. "Did you see the look on her face? God, to think I used to fear that woman."

Ava remained standing, her hands on her hips as she seemed to study her.

"What?"

"You do realize you just stood up to one of the most influential women in the state of New York?"

Harriet considered it, recalling how months before, she'd circled the date of the McCarthy benefit on her calendar. Though she hadn't attended an event in some time, she'd been compelled to act as if such things were still the pinnacle of importance. So much had happened since then, and there was so much else to the world. She laughed again. "I'm going to have to call Mother. She won't believe me for a moment."

Ava returned to the bench. When Harriet collected herself, she found Ava watching her. The look in her eyes held a mixture of things: admiration, surprise, and a gentle question Harriet had longed to see. It was a question she used to know the answer to. She swallowed, passing Ava her tea as she held her cup between them.

"To New York's elite," she said, smiling wide.

Ava's laughter was full and bright as they toasted to the life

Harriet had always known, the life that had begun to distance itself from her. She felt ready now to let it be, watching it go with Martha back down the path and into the depths of upper Manhattan. And as her old life fell away, Harriet started to see what lay ahead for her and just how bright that future could be. Maybe, she thought with a glance at Ava, even brighter than she could imagine.

CHAPTER TWENTY-THREE

They spent the following days going over the appraiser's list.

"This is better than I expected," Harriet said, eyeing the multi-page list next to her plate of eggs. "He underpriced the second Rembrandt, but everyone thinks that one's a copy. I was there, though, when Father bought it from the British Museum."

Ava nodded. If she stared at the list too long, her head spun. Financially, she'd always been somewhere between hard times and nearly comfortable. The numbers next to the Browning auction items were staggering. She couldn't begin to imagine how much Harriet owed the bank if this would only leave her a little extra. Permitting everything sold, of course.

That weekend, Harriet went downstairs to drop the invitations in the building's outgoing mail. Ava was in the office, still in her robe at eleven in the morning. She was searching for her preferred fountain pen in order to add to Harriet's latest grocery list. Not finding it, she wandered back to her room in case she'd mislaid it there. Sifting through the contents of her handbag, she found her parents' letter.

"I forgot I put this in here." She'd been so caught up in finishing the invitations and the influx of hope after their encounter with Martha that Ava had felt like she was floating on a fast-moving cloud. Details of life before the park had drifted to the background of her mind.

Her father's handwriting tugged her back to reality as she sat on the bed to read.

Hi, honey.

Summer was kind to us. Crops are looking good. They put in a movie theater on Main Street. Gonna take your mother to see that Jimmy Stewart film. Car needs some work, but I'll get it fixed up. It's yours to use whenever you come back for a visit.

We know you're busy. I bet the mail room has you on your feet day and night. Your mother likes to imagine a new restaurant you eat at each weekend. Still can't hardly believe you're off in the big city. I know, you've been there a long time now. You always did go after your dreams. You never let your brothers or us tell you what to do.

We miss you, but we know you're living those dreams.

All our love, Dad and Mom.

Ava brought a knee to her chest as she reread the final sentences. For so long, she hadn't wanted to write back. It had been easier that way, easier to let her parents believe what they wanted. She balled her free fist. No, what *she* wanted. She wanted them to have the image of her thriving. She had wanted to seem like everything was great, even when it wasn't.

As her brothers had disappeared, she'd thought clinging to the stagnant image she had created for herself among the bright lights was a gift to her parents. Give them something good, she had told herself. It was what she'd said each time she hadn't picked up a pen, each time she'd put one of their letters in a drawer. But what might have started with good intentions had morphed. Ava clutched her stomach, guilt twisting her insides at how selfish she'd been. She'd held on to so much, but it was doing more harm than good. Her parents deserved better. She hadn't been living her dreams. She hadn't been going after what she wanted.

Her head lifted at the sound of the elevator. Dreams she didn't even know she could have again, that was what she needed to go after.

What was she waiting for with Harriet? For her to say she was sorry for what had happened in college? They'd already had that conversation. They'd already lit the fire. What was she afraid of?

"I'm expecting an important call," Harriet said, sounding breathless from her errand, in the hallway. Seconds later, she appeared in the door. "Father's financial advisors need to talk." Her smile seemed to brighten the room. When she noticed the letter, it faltered. "What's that?"

Ava shifted to sit cross-legged. "A letter from home."

Harriet's face turned serious. "Is everything all right?"

"They're fine." Ava sniffled. She smiled at Harriet's perfect posture, one hand on her hip, a small line of concern at the edge of her lips. Ava wanted to go to her, to let Harriet hold her forever. "Harriet, we should talk."

Her hand fell to her side, and she straightened. "Oh?" Ava smiled, trying to seem encouraging. "All right." She moved to sit when the telephone rang. They both turned at the sound. After the second ring, Harriet bit her lip but stayed sitting.

Ava shook her head. "Go on."

"But—"

"You said you were expecting an important call."

"Ava—" Harriet reached out. In her touch, Ava felt it.

Harriet was willing to let it ring. She was willing to let the men on the other end of the line wait. She was willing to ignore them for her.

"Go, Harriet. We'll talk soon." She smiled.

Harriet looked worried but nodded and hurried down the hall. Ava watched her go, then looked back at the letter. She found the pen in her handbag, then went back to the office in search of stationery. She had a letter to write.

❖

Not three seconds after Harriet hung up the phone, it rang again.

"What is this, Grand Central Station?" She kept her hand on the receiver, inhaling deeply and bracing herself for whatever Mr. Gray had forgotten to mention. She didn't think there could be anything else. She'd told them the appraiser's numbers and how, if all went as she hoped at the auction, she'd have enough to climb out of the gaping financial hole her father had left. She was taken aback when her mother's voice came over the line.

"Harriet, what's this about an auction? Martha McCarthy telephoned two days ago in an absolute fit."

"I rang you about this last night, Mother. Your maid said you were out."

"Buck and I were at his cabin in Phoenix. We got back early this morning."

Harriet sighed, then told her about the meeting with Martha in the park.

"Harriet, you do understand with whom you were speaking? That woman has run every Ladies Council in New York City since, well, the nineteenth century."

Harriet rolled her eyes. Her bun felt too tight on the back

of her head, and she worked to loosen it as she spoke. "She's also the woman who wore a cape to Father's funeral."

Her mother snorted, but her tone remained worried. "I'm only concerned about you and how this will be perceived."

How I'll be perceived, more like. Harriet only scoffed. It was so easy for her mother—her beautiful, revered mother—to quip about the workings of America's upper echelons from the safety of the distant desert.

Her conversation with Scarlett echoed in her mind, and Harriet took a deep breath and grabbed the end of her desk to steady herself. *Be brave.* "Mother, you're not here. You haven't been here in years."

"I haven't lost touch, if that's what you're implying. Cynthia Smith sends me the *New York Post* each month. The ladies telephone. I'm well aware of what's happening in my old world."

"Are you? Are you aware that your daughter hasn't been seen at an event in over a year? That she's been trapped inside your Manhattan apartment, too afraid of what everyone would say if they saw the poor heiress wandering the city, no husband, no father, no money."

"Harriet—"

"Mother, you've no idea what it's been like." Harriet pinched the bridge of her nose. "Perhaps I should have called more. But the truth is what you heard. I'm hosting the final Browning event New York City will ever see in just a few weeks. And frankly, I don't care anymore what Martha McCarthy or Susie Astor or Will Forbes says about me." She swallowed hard, her body fighting the next confession that slipped from her lips. "I haven't been happy, Mother. Not in a long time."

The line was quiet. "Sweetheart, I didn't know."

"I didn't want you to know. You're off galivanting with

Buck like a scene from a movie. I didn't want you or anybody to ever see me as anything other than capable of handling whatever came my way. But eventually, I had to admit I needed help." She paused. "Ava has been working for me. She's helping to organize the auction."

"Ava?" Her mother fell quiet. Harriet imagined the frown drooping her rouged cheeks, her painted nails tapping the nearest surface as she combed her memories. "The young woman from Briarcliff?"

"Yes. Ava Clark. She, well, I don't know what I would have done without her."

After a time, her mother asked, "Where will you go? After, I mean. You're welcome here. Buck would love to see you again."

Harriet laughed, knowing she meant that as, "I would like to see you," but that wasn't how Velma Browning worked. "I'm considering the house in San Francisco. I could help oversee the mills in the Northwest." *It's also as far as I can get from this place without falling into the ocean.*

"What about Lawrence?"

"Mother."

"Scarlett, then. Won't you miss her?"

"Scarlett knows she can hop on a train any day she likes."

It was quiet a time before the faint sound of spurs jangling came from her mother's side of the line. "Buck heading out?"

"We both are. We have a ride scheduled."

"You could be a stuntwoman in a western at this point."

Her mother laughed. "I think you're right. Do try to visit, sweetheart. I…I know I wasn't there. I haven't been there. Buck showed me another world. And after your father died, well, the glitz of the city lost its glam."

Harriet nodded, understanding.

"But the way you've stayed strong all this time. Well, I'm

very proud of you." The unfamiliar words took any retort from Harriet. Her mother called to someone on the other side of the phone, then said, "Good luck. Call me once it's over. Love you, darling."

Harriet could barely say, "I love you, too," before the line disconnected.

CHAPTER TWENTY-FOUR

The night before the auction, Ava was in bed by nine. They'd been so busy all day, preparing the apartment to host what, according to the RSVP list, was nearly fifty attendees to the H. Browning estate auction.

Harriet had seemed calm, if occupied, all day. There was a steady undercurrent of pride in each of her movements. Ava, it turned out, was the anxious one as they reached only one more night between her and the beginning of the end.

She tried not to think about how little time she had left here. She still hadn't talked to Harriet since the other day. Organizing the apartment for the auction, preparing the food and drink, and going over the items to be sold had occupied every free moment. She did still have a job to do, after all.

She'd fallen asleep and opened her eyes to the dark figure of Harriet crawling into bed with her. "What time is it?"

"Nearly midnight," Harriet said, pulling Ava closer, wrapping an arm around her waist.

"Everything perfect?"

Harriet chuckled. "Hardly. But I do feel ready." She yawned.

"Good." Ava kissed her forehead, and Harriet snuggled closer. All evidence they'd been sharing a room would be gone by breakfast. The auction started at 11:00, and nobody would know just how much time they were spending together. *Or how much more time I want*, Ava thought.

"Harriet?" She felt Harriet's already steady breathing.

"Hmm?"

"Nothing. It can wait." Ava wasn't sure it could, but Harriet was in her arms. Right now, that was what mattered.

The next morning leapt upon them in a flurry. Harriet was up at the first sign of dawn, and Ava did her best to keep up.

"Scarlett will be here at ten thirty to help with final touches."

"I wouldn't be surprised if she showed up with Imogene," Ava added, smoothing her hair in the bathroom mirror.

Harriet's reply sounded farther away, no doubt on her way to the kitchen. "Peas in a pod, those two."

Ava laughed. Lowering her hand, she studied her reflection, then the room. Harriet had begun to pack. A couple boxes peeked out from behind her wardrobe. Ava rested her elbows on the vanity table, then lightly touched each of the stoppers in Harriet's perfumes and lotions. She smiled, recalling the days she wore the rose water and when she opted for the lavender scent.

Rediscovering Harriet was something she'd grown to love. A sharp sinking feeling gripped her stomach, and she met her own gaze in the mirror. She was hit with a reminder of what would happen when this was done. Her dark, empty apartment waited on the other side of town. Piles of want ads loomed as another job search reared its head. Mr. Wakowski lingered near, chewing on a lemon bar, eager to fill his pockets with rent money. Taking a deep breath, she leaned against the vanity. She could deal with all of that if she had to, but could she give Harriet up again?

A short while later, Scarlett arrived. Imogene was not

with her, which Ava wasn't completely surprised by. Neither was Harriet, which Ava was glad for.

"I know I'm not her favorite person," Harriet muttered in the kitchen, passing Ava more finger sandwiches to arrange on a silver tray for guests.

"She'll come around eventually," Ava replied. Harriet looked thoughtful, and Ava realized her comment implied a future in which Imogene had time to forgive Harriet. Ava licked her lips, a feeling like wings beating in her chest, making the words stick in her throat. The sound of chairs being moved across the carpet in the library told her Scarlett was still busy. She opened her mouth but still couldn't speak. Ava couldn't bring herself to put her heart out there again. As fervent as the beating wings rang in her body, the scars on her heart seemed to squeeze tight, begging her to remember them.

She only smiled. "I'll take these." She grabbed the tray. She felt Harriet watching her. Ava could feel the line drawing them together tighten as she walked away.

It gave a sudden jerk, however, when Harriet said, "Come with me."

Ava nearly dropped the tray in the doorway. She closed her eyes. It could be a dream, a vision, her desires screaming so loud that they sounded real. But when Harriet spoke again, the truth called her back to earth.

"Ava, come with me."

Slowly, she turned. Harriet stood before the sink. Her elegant but subdued day dress was a soft blue, matching her eyes, which looked at Ava in the way they had last night. Full of passion, yearning, and love. "I want you—" Her voice broke, and she gave a small laugh. Ava tightened her grip on the tray so as not to drop it. "I want you to come with me when all this is done. I don't want this to end."

The air seemed thick, heady, and Ava felt like she was floating. Tears gathered at the corners of her vision. She smiled.

"What do you say?" Harriet asked, her voice hushed.

"Harriet—"

"I hear the elevator, girls. We better—" Scarlett swung into the doorway, her words falling short as her eyes grew wide. She glanced between them. "My, it's hot as dickens in here. Did I interrupt something?"

Ava, somehow managing to tear her gaze from Harriet's, shook her head. "I was just taking these out."

Scarlett raised a brow, then moved to pick up a dessert tray.

Over her shoulder, Ava smiled at the look of hope in Harriet's eyes. Her words had done what Ava hadn't thought possible. They'd washed away the apprehension of what lay beyond the auction. Her worries were swept up in the fierceness of Harriet's bright gaze, tossed aside, leaving only enough room for what Ava had believed was an unattainable possibility: the chance of a life with Harriet.

❖

Harriet stood at the front of the room. She looked out over the small sea of perfectly coiffed heads and breathed in the air, musty and muddled with too many perfumes. The shifting of low heels against the floor was the only sound. Eventually, she tore her gaze from the point on the carpet she'd fixed on and met the curious, vying eyes of the elite women of New York. Some came to show their support or sympathy, no doubt having followed the headlines over the last few years. Others, meanwhile, had come to refill their bejeweled handbags with enough gossip to take back with them to their mansions.

The pile of newspaper clippings called to her from the

desk drawer across the room. She thought holding on to those—keeping the jabs and gossip close—was driving her forward, willing her to succeed. Really, they'd kept her back, latching her to a life that wasn't real anymore, that wasn't hers. Like most of the people in the room today. These weren't her people, not anymore. Most had come to bear witness to the end of the Brownings in New York. If it wasn't clear to them already, the reality of Harriet's circumstances would be evident in the soon-to-be vacant penthouse. Then it would be unavoidable, impossible to hide the financial distress, the need to go, the disappearing act of another family fortune to the changing times.

After meeting several of their eager gazes, Harriet found Ava at the back of the room. Her eyes seemed to smile. Harriet exhaled.

She knew what these people would think, what they perceived: a downtrodden heiress fleeing the city, unable to withstand the social fall she'd taken. But Harriet knew that wasn't what was happening. Ava and Scarlett, those she cared about most, knew that, too. No, Harriet Browning wasn't running away. She was breaking free, striking her own path. *Even if Ava won't accompany me, I'll do it. I'll make my way.*

Breaking her gaze from Ava's, she couldn't help but think how nice it would be to have somebody to start anew with. Her mother had done it, had escaped the city and found love. Harriet clenched her fists, then forced them open again, willing the hope of a future with Ava out across the room, hoping she could feel it. Hoping she wanted it, too.

Straightening, she cleared her throat, smiled, and said, "Welcome, everyone, to the Browning estate auction. Let's begin."

CHAPTER TWENTY-FIVE

"Have another glass of water, H. Your voice will be a toad's song tomorrow if you don't." Scarlett handed her the glass, then plopped next to her on the office couch.

"Thanks, Scar," Harriet said, kicking off her heels and resting them on the coffee table's edge. "I fear it's my feet that will be feeling it tomorrow. I knew I was out of practice when it comes to being on my feet at an event, but"—she took a long drink—"my dogs are barking, as they say."

"Your...what?" Scarlett asked, one hand on her forehead as she leaned back, her eyes closed.

Across the room, Ava snorted.

Harriet frowned over her glass. "Did I say it wrong?"

"You said it right." Ava smiled.

"I used to be so keen on the latest lingo," Scarlett mused. "Ava, darling, you must teach me the working woman's words."

Ava and Harriet laughed. "Hasn't Imogene shared her knowledge?"

"Oh, sure, but I wish to know all. I may be a Manhattanite, but one can never believe themselves above their fellow woman."

"Hear, hear," Harriet said, raising her water. While

Scarlett rehashed the afternoon's events, gushing over which items everyone purchased, Harriet kept her gaze toward Ava. She was dying to know her thoughts. No, her answer. She'd meant every word of her invitation. She couldn't imagine life without Ava. Even if it was as friends or companions. Of course, she wanted more, but Harriet would take whatever Ava was willing to give her.

The sun was down when Harriet walked Scarlett to the elevator. "Thanks again, Scar, for everything." They hugged.

Scarlett donned her hat and grabbed her handbag. "Telephone me before you leave, you hear? I know you've got a week or so, but..." She smiled, and Harriet was surprised at the tears in her eyes.

"I will," she said, squeezing Scarlett's hand. "We'll do tea."

Scarlett seemed unable to find her words as Harriet pulled open the elevator gate for her. Closing it, Scarlett turned. She nodded at something behind Harriet, toward the office. "Be good to that one. She's a gem."

"I will."

Scarlett smiled and was gone. For a moment, Harriet stood, staring at the golden bars of the elevator cage. Only now did she see the tarnish on their edges, the faded gleam. It wasn't like it once was. Not much was. But, she thought, perhaps that wasn't a bad thing.

Turning, she cried out at Ava coming up the hallway behind her. "Ava, you startled—" She couldn't finish her sentence before Ava was kissing her, wrapping her arms around her. Harriet met her actions, returning the fervent kiss and pulling Ava closer. When Harriet broke for air, she could only search Ava's face for an explanation.

"I've been dying to kiss you all evening. Through the auction. Harriet, you were brilliant. I know that couldn't have been easy." She searched her gaze, then said, "I'm so proud of you."

The words kick-started a spark in Harriet's chest that spread like a fuse through her body. She could feel her smile stretch wide as she cupped Ava's face. She started to lean in again when Ava grabbed her hand.

"Come with me." She led Harriet into their room. From the side table drawer, Ava pulled out a pair of letters. Harriet turned on the light and sat beside Ava on the bed. "This is from the US Navy headquarters in London." She handed Harriet the letter. "I've written them every other month for years. Ever since James went missing."

Harriet pulled out the letter, scanning the formal, stiff language.

"I hadn't even fully grieved William before James followed him into the fog. It seemed impossible. Unfair." Ava took a breath. "This is the last one. James is gone. Both of them..." Her voice broke, and she pursed her lips.

Harriet reached out, resting a hand on Ava's knee. Years ago, she would have felt the need to counter Ava's grief with words, empty phrases that couldn't truly soothe her ache. Now, she knew what Ava needed was her presence, knowing she was there and always would be in times of heartache.

Wiping her face, Ava took a deep breath. "I can't forget the past." She glanced at Harriet, her eyes gleaming, "but I have to move forward." She gave a small laugh. "James would kick my backside if he saw me wallowing for as long as I have."

"He did have a certain zest for life."

"He did." Ava turned, pulling one leg closer to face her. "He would want me to continue on, and I'm finally ready to. Harriet, being with you wasn't something I expected to want again. I'm still..." She glanced down. "I'm still a little afraid."

Frowning, Harriet took her hands. "Of what?"

Ava looked up, her gaze wide and questioning. "I'm afraid of what happens if this is right. What happens if this is everything I hoped it could be?"

Harriet felt ready to burst at the anticipation in Ava's eyes. "Ava. I'm afraid, too. But not of this." She pulled their hands to her chest, resting them over her heart. "I regret making the choices I did all those years ago. But I think perhaps that was because someone like God, the universe, whatever you care to call it, knew I wasn't ready. I loved you utterly at Briarcliff, but I was weak in my love. I've had time to build myself into somebody who can hold her head high, even when it seems easier to hide. And even though, now, I don't have much money, or much of a reputation, for that matter—"

Ava laughed. "You know that never mattered to me."

"I do. I did. I just…" Harriet licked her lips, searching for the right words. "I don't want to disappoint you. I don't want to ever hide, not with you. I love you, Ava Clark, and if you decide to come with me, I'll spend every day reminding you of that love. I'll show you I'll always be there."

Seconds passed or maybe hours. Harriet couldn't tell. The entire span of time might have encompassed them in that moment, expanding and bending in upon itself. Time seemed unimportant as Ava looked at her, hope and love pushing out into the space between them until Ava leaned in, kissing her.

Harriet smiled, asking, "Is that a yes? Will you come with me?"

Ava smiled into another kiss, then said, "Yes, Harriet Browning. I would love to."

EPILOGUE

I think we have everything," Ava said, scanning her surroundings, hands on her hips.

"Don't forget the food basket," Harriet called from the hallway.

Ava laughed. "You know they serve food on the train?"

"It's always good to have sustenance in case of emergencies," she called back.

Shaking her head, Ava finished her sweep of the kitchen and grabbed the picnic basket from the counter. She took in the polished appliances, the empty shelves. Momentarily, she fell back into the memory of moments with Harriet: that day when Harriet had been crouched on the floor, completely disheveled, a broken dish scattered on the floor; the night after July Fourth, when she'd taken care of Harriet, afraid she'd made a mistake, pushing her too far.

We've lived a full life inside these walls. Then she smiled, knowing there was another life waiting for them just outside.

In the hallway, she found Harriet looking frazzled but beautiful in a deep green day dress and low heels. She placed her suitcase near the elevator. "Mother says to call once we're headed south in a few weeks. Buck needs time to prepare his deer jerky. I'm afraid to know what that is."

Ava chuckled, pulling Harriet by the waist and kissing her. "I'll remind you, don't worry." Harriet's body relaxed beneath her touch.

Pulling back, she said, "Scarlett already has a ticket for February."

"I'm not surprised in the least."

"Did Mr. Wakowski get the recipe you left him?"

Ava nodded. "He did. That was the first time I saw the man almost smile. He loves those lemon bars."

Harriet stepped back, her shoes echoing on the hardwood floors. All the rugs had been rolled up, hauled into a storage container and shipped with the pieces of furniture Harriet had readied for their move. They weren't taking much, only the things left after the auction. Her mother's old vanity, a few of Harriet's father's possessions, and their bed. The rest had gone, distributed throughout the city. The items of a once prestigious family drifting among the rest of New York's society.

They both stood and took in the empty walls, the hush that fell over a place that used to be a home.

"How was the call with Mr. Gray this morning?" Ava asked, handing Harriet her hat as she called up the elevator.

"Good. I have one more payment to make, but the majority of the debt is settled. Thank goodness."

"Thanks to you," Ava said, giving her an encouraging smile.

Harriet nodded. "Thanks to us." She hesitated, then added, "You're sure you won't mind taking that bookkeeping job in the mill outside the city?" Ava squeezed her hand, loving the concern in her voice. "We have enough to get by, at least for a while."

"I don't mind, truly," Ava said. "I'm a working woman, remember?" She grinned. "Besides, it will be fun coming home to you at the end of each day."

Harriet bit her lip. "All right. Well." She took a deep breath. "Like you said, all of this." She nodded to the room. "It's done."

"And you're ready?" Ava asked. "For the next step?" She swallowed, realizing she was asking not only for Harriet but for herself. As quickly as she asked it, though, she knew the answer. She was absolutely ready to take this journey with Harriet, who matched her with a smile.

"I'm ready." Harriet grabbed her suitcase, and Ava opened the elevator gate. Inside, they met each other's gazes. "Are you ready to see your parents? We'll be in Pennsylvania by Tuesday."

Ava took a deep breath. "Honestly, I don't know. Having you by my side makes me feel a little less afraid." And that, Ava thought, was more than she could have ever wished for.

Harriet smiled. "And Imogene? Do you think she'll visit?"

Ava closed the elevator gate. "She said if I'm still living with you come June, she'll consider it."

"And will you still be with me come June?"

Ava grinned. "I'll have to check my calendar." She winked, then kissed Harriet as the elevator cable rumbled to a start. "I have a good feeling, though."

Laughing, Harriet kissed her deeply as, for the last time, they held on to one another in Harriet's Manhattan apartment. As the button light came on, signaling their arrival in the lobby, Ava took Harriet's hand.

"Shall we?"

Harriet beamed, leading the way. "We shall."

About the Author

Originally from Dallas-Ft. Worth, Sam Ledel has worked in education for ten years. She enjoys being able to write in her free time and is currently working on her next novel.

Books Available From Bold Strokes Books

Closed-Door Policy by Erin Zak. Going back to college is never easy, but Caroline Stevens is prepared to work hard and change her life for the better. What she's not prepared for is Dr. Atlanta Morris, her gorgeous new professor. (978-1-63679-181-4)

Homeworld by Gun Brooke. Headed by Captain Holly Crowe, the spaceship Velocity's crew journeys toward their alien ancestors' homeworld, and what they find is completely unexpected—and they're not safe. (978-1-63679-177-7)

Outland by Kristin Keppler & Allisa Bahney. Danielle Clark and Katelyn Turner can't seem to stay away from one another even as the war for the wastelands tests their loyalty to each other and to their people. (978-1-63679-154-8)

Royal Exposé by Jenny Frame. When they're grouped together for a class assignment, Poppy's enthusiasm for life and love may just save Casey's soul, but will she ever forgive Casey for using her to expose royal secrets? (978-1-63679-165-4)

Secret Sanctuary by Nance Sparks. US Deputy Marshal Alex Trenton specializes in protecting those awaiting trial, but when danger threatens the woman she's falling for, Alex is in for the fight of her life. (978-1-63679-148-7)

Stranded Hearts by Kris Bryant, Amanda Radley & Emily Smith. In these novellas from award-winning authors, fate intervenes on behalf of love when characters are unexpectedly stuck together. With too much time and an irresistible attraction, anything could happen. (978-1-63679-182-1)

The Last Lavender Sister by Melissa Brayden. Aster Lavender sells her gourmet doughnuts and keeps a low profile; she never plans on the town's temporary veterinarian swooping in and making her feel like anything but a wallflower. (978-1-63679-130-2)

The Probability of Love by Dena Blake. As Blair and Rachel keep ending up in the same place despite the odds, can a one-night stand turn into forever? Or will the bet Blair never intended to make ruin their happily ever after? (978-1-63679-188-3)

Worth a Fortune by Sam Ledel. After placing a want ad for a personal secretary, a New York heiress is surprised when the woman who got away is the one interested in the position. (978-1-63679-175-3)

A Fox in Shadow by Jane Fletcher. Cassie's mission is to add new territory to the Kavillian empire—murder, betrayal, war, and the clash of cultures ensue. (978-1-63679-142-5)

Embracing the Moon by Jeannie Levig. Just as Gwen and Taylor are exploring the new love they've found, the present and past collide, threatening the future they long to share. (978-1-63555-462-5)

Forever Comes in Threes by D. Jackson Leigh. Efficiency expert Perry Chandler's ordered life is upended when she inherits three busy terriers, and the woman she's referred to for help turns out to be her bitter podcast rival, the very sexy Dr. Ming Lee. (978-1-63679-169-2)

Missed Conception by Joy Argento. Maggie Walsh wants a relationship with Cassidy, the daughter she's only just discovered she has due to an in vitro mix-up. Heat kindles between Maggie and Cassidy's mother in a way neither expects. (978-1-63679-146-3)

Private Equity by Elle Spencer. Cassidy Bennett spends an unexpected evening at a lesbian nightclub with her notoriously reserved and demanding boss, Julia. After seeing a different side of Julia, Cassidy can't seem to shake her desire to know more. (978-1-63679-180-7)

Racing the Dawn by Sandra Barrett. After narrowly escaping a house fire, vampire Jade Murphy is unexpectedly intrigued by gorgeous firefighter Beth Jenssen, and her undead existence might just be perking up a bit. (978-1-63679-271-2)

Reclaiming Love by Amanda Radley. Sarah's tiny white lie means somehow convincing Pippa to pretend to be her girlfriend. Only the more time they spend faking it, the more real it feels. (978-1-63679-144-9)

Forever by Kris Bryant. When Savannah Edwards is invited to be the next bachelorette on the dating show *When Sparks Fly*, she'll show the world that finding true love on television can happen. (978-1-63679-029-9)